THE MYSTERY
OF THE
MEMORIAL DAY FIRE

TRIXIE BELDEN®

The TRIXIE BELDEN Series

1 The Secret of the Mansion
2 The Red Trailer Mystery
3 The Gatehouse Mystery
4 The Mysterious Visitor
5 The Mystery Off Glen Road
6 The Mystery in Arizona
7 The Mysterious Code
8 The Black Jacket Mystery
9 The Happy Valley Mystery
10 The Marshland Mystery
11 The Mystery at Bob-White Cave
12 The Mystery of the Blinking Eye
13 The Mystery on Cobbett's Island
14 The Mystery of the Emeralds
15 The Mystery on the Mississippi
16 The Mystery of the Missing Heiress
17 The Mystery of the Uninvited Guest
18 The Mystery of the Phantom Grasshopper
19 The Secret of the Unseen Treasure
20 The Mystery Off Old Telegraph Road
21 The Mystery of the Castaway Children
22 The Mystery at Mead's Mountain
23 The Mystery of the Queen's Necklace
24 The Mystery at Saratoga
25 The Sasquatch Mystery
26 The Mystery of the Headless Horseman
27 The Mystery of the Ghostly Galleon
28 The Hudson River Mystery
29 The Mystery of the Velvet Gown
30 The Mystery of the Midnight Marauder
31 The Mystery at Maypenny's
32 The Mystery of the Whispering Witch
33 The Mystery of the Vanishing Victim
34 The Mystery of the Missing Millionaire
35 The Mystery of the Memorial Day Fire
36 The Mystery of the Antique Doll
37 The Pet Show Mystery
38 The Indian Burial Ground Mystery
39 The Mystery of the Galloping Ghost

TRIXIE BELDEN®

THE MYSTERY
OF THE
MEMORIAL DAY FIRE

By Kathryn Kenny

Black-and-white illustrations by Jim Spence

A GOLDEN BOOK • NEW YORK

Western Publishing Company, Inc., Racine, Wisconsin 53404

Contents

1   The Torchlight Parade   9

2   Retreat to Crabapple Farm   25

3   A Meeting of the Bob-Whites   39

4   "Arson!"   53

5   A Trip to Jail   62

6   At the Scene of the Crime   73

7   Trixie Has a Plan   87

8   One Clue Lost . . . One Clue Found   102

9   Selling and Sleuthing   119

10   Was It a Payoff?   133

11   "We're Going to the Police!"   144

12   The Right Suspect   160

13   Who, What, When, Where, and Why   173

1 ∗ The Torchlight Parade

"OH, HONEY, AREN'T PARADES WONDERFUL?" Trixie Belden didn't wait for an answer, because she knew her best friend would agree. "I just love the clowns and the horses and the marching bands." Trixie's blue eyes were shining, and her cheeks glowed under their dusting of freckles. Her sandy blond curls, which always bounced when she was excited, were practically dancing.

"My sororal sibling has particularized a procession that has not yet commenced," Mart Belden said, rolling his own blue eyes upward in a look of mock-disbelief. Mart was Trixie's "almost twin," just eleven months older and with the same sandy hair and freckles. He used his almost-constant teasing to hide his deep affection for his younger sister.

"I *think* he means that you just described the parade even though it hasn't started yet," Honey Wheeler told Trixie. Both of the girls loved to decipher Mart's inflated sentences, to show him he wasn't the only smart one in their group. "But I don't see what's so strange about that, since the Sleepyside-on-the-Hudson Memorial Day Torchlight Parade is always the same, every single year. That's what I love about it — that and getting to see absolutely everyone in town lined up along Main Street to watch." Honey's hazel eyes were shining, too, and the cool breeze made her honey-blond shoulder-length hair look pleasantly windblown.

Jim Frayne put his arm around Honey's shoulders and gave his adopted sister an affectionate hug. "I can't believe there was ever a time in my life when I didn't spend Memorial Day eve watching the parade on Main Street," he said.

"I can't, either," Dan Mangan agreed.

"I *have* spent every Memorial Day watching this parade," Di Lynch said. "But I can't believe I didn't always watch it with the other Bob-Whites of the Glen."

"Well, at least we're all together *this* year," Brian Belden observed in his reasonable way. "That's really all that matters." Brian, the oldest of the Beldens, was also the calmest and most logical.

Happily, Trixie nodded her agreement. The seven young people standing on the curb in the twilight were more than good friends. They were the total membership of a semisecret club called the Bob-Whites of the Glen, which was dedicated to helping others and to having fun.

The fun certainly included times like this, waiting together on Main Street for the Memorial Day parade to begin. But making the club a success had also required giving lots of help to one another, as well as to the community.

Not too long before, Jim Frayne had been a runaway, hiding from his cruel stepfather and having nowhere to turn after his great-uncle died. Then Jim had met Trixie and Honey, and Honey's parents had adopted him.

Dan Mangan, too, had once been without a real home. Instead of running away, Dan had gotten involved with a street gang in New York City, where he'd lived. His Uncle Regan, the Wheelers' groom, had brought Dan to Sleepyside to get him away from those bad companions.

Di Lynch had always lived in Sleepyside. Her life had changed, though, when her father suddenly made a lot of money and the Lynches moved into a luxurious mansion. Di had been confused and frightened by the change, but her friendship with Trixie and Honey had helped her to adjust.

Honey, too, had gone through her share of unhappiness to get to this Memorial Day parade. It was almost impossible to remember that the Honey Wheeler who had first come to live in Sleepyside had been thin and pale and afraid of her own shadow.

Honey's parents had always been wealthy. Her father was a hard-working businessman who traveled a lot. Her mother was loving but not very strong. As a result, Honey had lived at boarding schools and summer camps. That had left her feeling unloved and insecure.

The Wheelers had bought the Manor House, a mansion just west of the farmhouse where Trixie lived, to give Honey a more stable home. Their plan had succeeded beyond their hopes mainly because of the sturdy, fearless tomboy who lived next door. In fact, Honey's parents sometimes wondered if things hadn't gone *too* far, especially when Honey got involved in the mysteries that Trixie was always trying to solve.

"We're going to have a beautiful starry night," Trixie pointed out. "That will make the parade even better."

"Oh, it certainly will," Honey agreed. "There's nothing sadder than seeing everyone huddled at the curbs under umbrellas. Nobody talks or laughs, and everyone seems just miserable."

"At least negative atmospheric conditions permit intensive inhalations," Mart said with a frown. "The magnitude of this assemblage is over-whelming."

"The crowd is half the fun and you know it, Mart Belden," Trixie said. "It's just as Honey said — this is the one day of the year when you can see just about everyone."

"I don't see Moms and Dad and Bobby," Brian said, his eyes scanning the crowd. "I hope they got close enough so that Bobby will get a good view."

"Even if they don't, Bobby will charm his way to the front," Honey said.

Bobby was the fourth and youngest of the Belden siblings. Honey Wheeler, who had no younger brothers or sisters of her own, was devoted to the energetic six-year-old. Trixie loved him, too, but she was more likely than Honey to lose patience with his antics.

"Oh, look," Di Lynch said. "There's old Brom and Mrs. Vanderpoel."

The other Bob-Whites looked to where Di was pointing. Sure enough, the two old people were waiting for the parade with as much excitement as the teenagers across the street from them. Old Brom and Mrs. Vanderpoel had lived in the country near Sleepyside all their lives.

"Just think how many Memorial Day parades they've been to," Trixie said, her eyes widening at the thought. "Probably since the days when there were real torches to light the parade, instead of streetlights that make it bright as day."

"Isn't that Nick Roberts across the street?" Jim asked.

"That's Nick, all right," Trixie said. She raised her hand and waved, and Nick waved back.

"He's certainly friendlier now than he was when we first met him," Honey said. "Remember that day at the art fair?"

"I certainly do," Trixie said, wrinkling her nose. "I also remember how unfriendly he was when I told him we were going to sponsor a bikeathon to raise money for the art department at Sleepyside Junior-Senior High School. I thought he'd be happy about it, since he'd already told us how badly the art department needed money for supplies and equipment. Instead, he was downright rude!"

"There's no excuse for being rude, but Nick Roberts had an awful lot on his mind just then," Brian said. "His mother was in poor health and his father's business was failing. Not to mention the fact that Nick wanted to get into art school, but couldn't get enough experience because Sleepyside didn't have the equipment he needed."

"It does now," Jim said.

"I hope Nick doesn't stop doing his marvelous pen-and-ink drawings," Honey said. "He admitted he chose that medium because pen and ink and paper were the only supplies he could afford. But I can't imagine any piece of sculpture or pottery more beautiful than the drawing Nick did of the Manor House. That's how we first met him — when I saw that drawing at the art fair."

"The drawing of Crabapple Farm is just as beautiful," Trixie said. The old farmhouse where the Beldens lived wasn't as fancy as the Wheeler mansion, but it was just as well loved by the people who lived there. "Moms loved it when I gave her the drawing for Mother's Day. It's a good thing I didn't keep it for myself, although I'd planned to until you said you were buying the picture of the Manor House for *your* mother." Trixie sighed. "I'll never be as generous as you are, Honey."

"It took a generous person to come up with the idea of having a bikeathon to raise money for art supplies," Jim said. "If it weren't for you, Trixie, Nick would still be doing only pen and ink — and not by choice."

Trixie felt herself starting to blush, as she often did when anyone paid her a compliment. Having the compliment come from Jim made the blush even deeper. All the Bob-Whites knew about the special feelings that Jim and Trixie had for one another, even though Trixie denied it and both of the young people tried not to show it.

"Well, I'm not responsible for the end of all of Nick's troubles," Trixie said quickly. "Look — the woman he's standing next to must be his mother. That means her health has improved. I'm sure that's a load off Nick's mind."

"I've heard his father's business has improved, too," Jim said. "Mr. Roberts is a master engraver, you know, and he was trying to get by with trophies and plaques and things that needed engraving. Now he's added caps and T-shirts, which are more in demand."

"There's Mr. Roberts now," Di said as a dark,

heavy-set man joined Nick and his mother. "He must have dropped them off and gone to park the car."

"Maybe he was working late, if business is as good as Jim says. His shop is just a couple of blocks from here," Trixie said. "I was there once, remember?"

"Remember who was responsible for the salvation of your epidermis prior to the bikeathon?" Mart asked mockingly.

"Now *that's* worth remembering," Jim said to Trixie. "I'm proud of you for helping Nick and his family, but I wish you hadn't got mixed up in a mystery — and a dangerous situation — along the way."

"Solving that mystery was just as important to Nick's future as the bikeathon itself," Honey said, jumping in as always to defend her fellow detective. Honey liked mysteries as much as Trixie did, and the two girls planned to start the Belden-Wheeler Detective Agency when they finished school.

"That's all right, Honey," Trixie said with a wave of her hand. "Jim and Mart made their point. But let's not talk about mysteries right now, because there isn't a mystery in sight. There *is* a parade in sight, though. Look!"

Trixie pointed down the street, and the Bob-Whites could see, blocks away, the satin banner of the first of the marching bands. At the same time, the first thin, clear notes of the glockenspiel sounded over the lower-pitched babel of the crowd.

"Oooh!" Di Lynch squealed. She clapped her hands and jumped up and down like a happy child. The animation made her even more beautiful than usual, although her slim figure, violet eyes, and black hair were always the envy of Trixie and Honey. "Trixie's right — it's starting! Oh, I can't wait, I can't wait!"

The chatter among the young people ended abruptly. All seven of them stared intently toward the beginning of the parade, with various looks of excitement and pure joy on their faces.

A sudden flash of light made Trixie's head snap back and her eyes snap closed. When she opened her eyes again, a huge blue spot was swimming in front of them. "Hey!" she said irritably. "What was that?"

"It's called a flash," said a sarcastic female voice. "It's used for taking pictures after dark."

Straining to see around the blue spot, Trixie looked in the direction of the voice. Sure enough, the young woman who had spoken was holding an expensive-looking camera with a flash attachment mounted on it.

"I'm Jane Dix-Strauss," the woman said, "reporter for the *Sleepyside Sun*. Can I have your names?"

Trixie felt her initial irritation growing. First the reporter had startled her, then she'd made fun of her for acting startled. Now she was acting as though nothing had happened. "What do you want our names for?" Trixie asked.

"So that I can print them in the paper under this picture. 'Sleepyside's young people turn out for annual parade,' that sort of thing." This time, Jane Dix-Strauss's voice sounded slightly bored, as if covering a parade in a small town was not her idea of exciting journalism.

As the spot faded from Trixie's eyes, she took a closer look at the reporter. Jane Dix-Strauss was small — not much taller than Trixie, and almost as slender as Honey. Her hair was dark and curly. She wore large-framed glasses, a spotless navy blue blazer with gold buttons, and a crisp tan cotton skirt. Everything about her looked intelligent, capable, and businesslike.

Self-consciously, Trixie's hand went to the missing button on the front of her red B.W.G. jacket. Honey had made the jackets for all the Bob-

Whites, and one of the club's membership requirements was to keep them looking spotless. Somehow, Trixie never succeeded. *I bet Jane Dix-Strauss always looks perfect*, Trixie thought irritably.

"I'm Di-Diana Lynch," said the young girl, who was almost as well dressed as Jane Dix-Strauss. "This is Mart Belden," she continued, giving the name of her favorite fellow Bob-White next. "This is Mart's brother Brian and that's their sister, Trixie. Or should I say Beatrix?"

"It's *Trixie*," the teenager said firmly. Just because her picture was going in the paper was no reason to remind everyone in town of her hated real name.

"I'm Honey Wheeler, and this is my brother, Jim Frayne," Trixie's friend said.

"Thanks," Jane Dix-Strauss said, putting a pencil and notepad back in the pocket of her blazer. "See you in the paper!"

"We're going to be in the paper!" Di exclaimed when the reporter had moved on. "I wonder how I looked when she took my picture."

"I'm sure you were beautiful, as usual, Di," Trixie said gloomily. "I'm bound to be the one with my mouth hanging open or my eyes half-closed. Although," she added, "my eyes must have been wide open this time, or that reporter couldn't have half-blinded me with her stupid flash."

"Now, Trixie," Honey said calmingly. "I know the flash was startling, but that's what makes a good newspaper picture — taking people by surprise."

"Then this picture will be great," Trixie said, refusing to be soothed even by her friend's honey-sweet disposition. "I just hope it's worth it to that reporter to be so rude."

"Your perspicuity in matters arcane is matched only by your predilection for prejudice, Beatrix," Mart said, adding extra sting to his remark by reminding Trixie again of the real name she'd been trying to forget since her first day of school.

"I'm not acting prejudiced about Jane Dix-Strauss," Trixie protested. "Prejudice is when you dislike someone you've never met. I've *met* her."

"You do tend to jump to conclusions about people, though, Trix," said Brian. "You jumped to the conclusion that Honey's cousin, Ben Riker, was trying to sabotage the bikeathon, for example. Remember?"

Suddenly humbled, and blushing yet again, Trixie nodded.

"Well, jumping to conclusions like that isn't a good idea," Brian said. "Keep an open mind about

Jane Dix-Strauss, okay? She was just doing her job as a reporter. When you see the picture of us in the paper tomorrow, you'll probably forget you were angry and start feeling grateful. I don't think there's another picture of all of us together. I hope we can get prints."

"That's a wonderful idea!" Honey said. "We can have a copy framed and hang it in our clubhouse."

Even Trixie had to brighten at that idea. The clubhouse was the pride and joy of every member of the Bob-Whites.

"You're right, Honey and Brian. I'm sorry." That was all Trixie had time to say, and even that short apology had to be shouted over the rattle of snare drums and the blare of cornets. The first of the marching bands was approaching the spot where the Bob-Whites were standing. The Memorial Day parade had really begun!

The band stopped right in front of Trixie and her friends to do a close-order drill that had them applauding. The band moved on, and a motorcyle drill team moved forward, doing such close figure eights that the handlebars of the big machines almost touched the ground.

After that came a group of clowns with colorful costumes and painted faces. The clowns tossed handfuls of candy into the crowd as they walked.

Forgetting their status as teenagers, the Bob-Whites jumped and scrambled for the candy. Trixie caught a root-beer barrel, which she immediately unwrapped and popped into her mouth — just in time to see Honey give the candy she'd caught to a small boy standing nearby.

Oh, woe, she thought. *Honey just finished being more understanding than I was about Jane Dix-Strauss, and now she's being more generous. When will I learn?*

Trixie's moment of regret was brief, though, because next in the parade were the Arabian horses. Honey and Trixie both loved horses and riding almost as much as they loved solving mysteries.

The Arabians — white, brown, and black — went by with prancing feet and plumelike tails. The silk tassels of their halters sparkled under the streetlights. The riders, in flowing robes of bright-colored satin, sat proudly on their mounts and waved at the crowd.

Trixie turned to follow the horses with her eyes until they were lost from sight. Then she turned back to watch the rest of the parade. If this year was like other years, it was no more than half over.

Suddenly, another bright light exploded in front of Trixie's eyes. Startled, she thought confusedly that another flash had gone off nearby.

But that thought only lasted a moment. The ball of orange flame was too huge to be a flash. The deafening boóm that came with it told the real story.

Somewhere off Main Street, something had just exploded!

2 * Retreat to Crabapple Farm

AFTER THE EXPLOSION, there were one or two seconds of what seemed to Trixie to be the deepest, stillest silence she'd ever heard — as though her heart itself had stopped beating.

Then, all at the same time, a dozen different noises began. Small children began to cry and older ones shrilled, "What was that? What made that noise?" Adults were asking one another the same question, and their voices added to the din.

Trixie could hear the terrified whinnying of horses down the street. She felt grateful that the horses were as far away as they were from the explosion, and that they were headed in the opposite direction.

Amid the commotion, Trixie suddenly realized that she could still hear the faint music of a marching band. Some valiant group was trying to carry on, in spite of the uproar. Even as she became aware of the music, though, it came to a ragged halt as one musician after another admitted defeat — or gave in to panic.

"What was it? What happened?" Honey asked in a hoarse whisper, as if she were reluctant to add any more to the noise around her.

Trixie had been so busy trying to get her bearings in the crowd that she'd almost forgotten the explosion itself. At Honey's question, she looked again in the direction from which the ball of fire and the deafening boom had come. As she looked, it seemed to her that she could still see a reddish glow in the darkening evening sky. She blinked her eyes and shook her head, wondering if the explosion had left a spot in front of her eyes just as Jane Dix-Strauss's flash had earlier.

Trixie opened her eyes and looked again. There was no doubt about it — the glow really was there. "Something exploded, Honey," Trixie said. "And now that something is on fire."

Although Honey, too, must have realized what had happened, hearing Trixie say it seemed to make it real for her. "Oh, no!" she moaned.

Trixie linked her arm through Honey's and leaned close to her, getting as well as giving support. She stood still, barely breathing, watching as the red glow grew brighter and listening to the excited, frightened hubbub of the crowd.

Then another noise was added — the cycling wail of the fire truck. Trixie breathed a sigh of relief when she recognized the sound, knowing that help was on the way. She stopped in mid-breath, though, when she realized that the wail of the truck had suddenly ceased to grow louder.

"Oh, no!" Trixie echoed Honey's moan. Sleepy-side's only fire station was on the opposite side of Main Street from the fire. The whole crowd of panicky, confused parade watchers stood in the way. The truck could not possibly get through!

Trixie stood frozen, looking from the red glow in the sky to the red cab of the fire truck, which she could see above the crowd. She looked from the truck back to the glow as if somehow, through sheer force of will, she could bring the two closer together.

She was roused from those useless, helpless thoughts by a rough hand on her shoulder. "Head for the car, Trixie," Brian Belden said to her. When his sister just looked at him dazedly, Brian repeated, "Go to the car, Trixie. Now! Move it!"

Trixie made her knees bend and her feet move through another effort of willpower. Honey, her arm still linked with Trixie's, moved along with her friend.

The action of her body cleared Trixie's mind, and she became really aware of the crowd for the first time since the explosion. There was fear on the faces of those around her, but there was also excitement, and most of the people she saw were heading *toward* the fire. That would only make the situation worse, she realized — as Brian had realized even sooner.

"Let's go," Dan said firmly. He had grasped Di's arm and pulled her, too, away from the confusion and toward the Bob-Whites' station wagon, which was parked several blocks from Main Street.

The four young people walked quickly, heads down. It was only after they'd gone almost a block that Trixie realized the other boys weren't with them.

She turned to look back and saw that Jim, Mart, and Brian were headed their way, but working slowly through the crowd, pleading with the spectators to clear the way. A few people, but not many, were responding to the boys' requests.

Trixie thought briefly of turning back to help her brothers and Jim. Then she decided that that would only make matters worse, starting a movement of people back toward the fire instead of away from it. She turned again toward the car and quickened her steps.

Trixie had never been so glad to see the station wagon with "Bob-Whites of the Glen" painted on the side. Her fear had grown in the moments since she had left Main Street. When she finally reached the car, her knees turned to jelly and she sat down abruptly on the curb.

Di Lynch suddenly burst into tears and stood sobbing softly against Dan Mangan's shoulder. Honey climbed into the car and sat, her back turned to Main Street and the fire, as if trying to block the whole thing from her mind.

Soon Jim and the two Beldens arrived at the station wagon. Jim climbed in behind the wheel and started the car. Mart, Brian, Dan, Di, and Trixie got in, and everyone rode to the Beldens' Crabapple Farm in silence.

Even after Jim had driven up the long drive and was parked next to the house, no one moved and no one spoke. Mart finally broke the silence when he yanked the door handle viciously and blurted, "Imbecilic pyrophiles!"

"You can say that again," Jim responded, shoving the gearshift lever into Park. He thumped the steering wheel with the heel of his hand for good measure. "Why won't people clear out at times like that?"

"Clear out?" Brian hooted. "What few people weren't on Main Street for the parade will *turn* out now that there's a fire to watch."

Trixie felt as awed by these bursts of temper as she had earlier by the burst of flame. A show of temper from Mart was no rarity, granted. But Brian Belden was almost always cool and calm. Jim Frayne had a temper that went with his red hair, but it took an awful lot to get him to show it.

She was quickly distracted from the boys' anger, though, as she crawled out of the station wagon and realized that it was the only vehicle in the driveway. "Moms and Dad and Bobby aren't home yet!" she exclaimed, a feeling of panic clutching at her stomach. She knew there was nothing to fear, really. Her parents and younger brother would have been standing *on* Main Street, watching the parade; the explosion had happened somewhere *off* Main Street. But still —

"Here they come," Brian said, pointing at the

maroon sedan that was coming down Glen Road. His voice sounded more relieved than reassuring, as though he, too, had felt a moment of fear.

The younger Beldens went into the comfortable old farmhouse, and their friends followed. There was no formal invitation given or asked for. Everyone realized they'd rather be together for a while.

Trixie went directly to the kitchen, opened the refrigerator, and took out a carton of milk. "I don't care if it's supposed to be spring," she said. "This whole thing has chilled me to the bone. I'm going to make some hot chocolate and melt about a million marshmallows in it."

"Oh, that sounds wonderful," Honey said gratefully. "Let me help you."

"Me, too," Di said.

"We'd better go call our parents first," Jim said. "News of the explosion might already be on the radio. They might be worried."

"Speaking of the radio," said Brian, "I'll tune in WSTH and see if there's any news."

"I'll help with the hot chocolate, Trixie," Dan said. "Honey and Jim will make sure my uncle knows I'm all right, and Mr. Maypenny won't know about the fire unless it's written up in next year's *Farmer's Almanac*."

In spite of herself, Trixie had to giggle at Dan's

statement. Mr. Maypenny was the gamekeeper for
the Wheeler game preserve. Dan lived with and
worked for the old man, whose tiny, rustic cabin
had no radio or television. Mr. Maypenny thought
newspapers and magazines caused people unnec-
essary worry, so he was unlikely to hear about the
fire very soon.

Before she could reply to Dan, the back door
burst open and Bobby Belden charged into the
kitchen. "Something exploded, Trixie. Didja hear
it, didja?" Not waiting for his sister's reply, Bobby
gave his impression of the noise: "*Ka-boom*! That
was what it sounded like, Trixie. *Ka-boom*! And
then there was a big red light, way up high in the
sky. And I said to Moms, 'You said this was Memorial Day, but Memorial Day isn't when they have
big lights in the sky. That's the Fourth of July!'
Isn't that right, Trixie?"

Trixie gave Dan a bewildered look over her
younger brother's head. As always, Bobby's state-
ments had a logic all their own. It was hard to
know where to start trying to explain to Bobby
what had happened.

Dan scooped the little boy up into his arms.
"You're right, Bobby. They do have big lights in
the sky on the Fourth of July. Those big lights are
called fireworks, and they're on purpose. The big

light we saw tonight was an accident. It wasn't part of Memorial Day. It just happened."

Bobby listened to the explanation solemnly. "Oh," he said. "Thanks for explaining, Dan." He wriggled out of Dan's arms and ran into the living room. "Something exploded, Brian," he shouted. "Didja hear it?"

Peter and Helen Belden were astonished when they walked into the kitchen a moment later and saw Trixie and Dan holding their stomachs, doubled over with hysterical laughter.

"Well," Peter Belden said, "I'm glad to see that you young people weren't too terribly frightened by the explosion."

"Oh, Daddy, we were," Trixie gasped through her giggles. "Really — I'm not — I'm not kidding. I think that's — that's why I'm l-laughing so h-hard right now."

"Let me guess," Helen Belden said. "Bobby ran in and gave you his Fourth of July speech."

Her mother's thoroughly accurate guess sent Trixie into another fit of giggling. "N-not only that, Moms. After Dan patiently explained the whole thing, Bobby ran off into the living room and started the whole thing over with Brian!"

Mrs. Belden nodded, smiling. "That's how children learn," she said. "The harder something is to understand, the more repetitions they need before they can grasp it."

Peter Belden shook his head, his dark eyes somber. "What happened tonight is hard even for me to grasp. I shouldn't wonder that it would take some time for Bobby to understand it." The serious look on his face was so much like the one his oldest son had been wearing a few minutes earlier that Trixie was struck again by how much Brian and his father looked alike. Both had dark eyes and dark, wavy hair. Both had a steady calmness.

"It was a horrible thing to happen," Mrs. Belden said. "It was the first time I can ever remember that the Memorial Day parade was stopped." Automatically, Helen Belden got out a plate and piled it with cookies from the cookie jar. Then she took out a tray and set out cups for the hot chocolate. Trixie noted with a grin that her mother had put out exactly the right number of cups, too — without even asking how many guests were in the house.

Trixie poured the chocolate, then Dan carried the tray into the living room while she followed with the plate of cookies.

Mart Belden fell upon the food eagerly, as always. "Ah, sustenance!" he exclaimed. "Succor!"

"These aren't suckers, Mart. They're *cookies*," Bobby said sternly.

"Delicious cookies they are, too, Mrs. Belden," Jim said, having picked up a cookie and a cup of cocoa on his way back from the telephone. "I don't know whether even these are enough to make me forget how stupidly people were behaving tonight, though."

Helen Belden's usually serene features suddenly looked stern. "I know exactly what you mean, Jim," she said. "We were standing right at the curb when the explosion happened, and we actually had to fight our way through the crowd to get away. Everyone else was headed toward the fire!"

"It's positively ghoulish!" Trixie said with a shudder.

"Not entirely," Mr. Belden said. "I agree with you that not clearing the way for the fire fighters is not very bright. I don't think that people mean any harm by it, though. I don't even think they flock toward the fire because they enjoy fires. I think it's more an attempt to take it all in, to understand it somehow. *Some* people," he added with a pointed look at Bobby, "do that by asking the same question over and over again. Other people do it by staying where they shouldn't be, hoping to look and listen long enough for it all to make sense."

There was a moment of silence when Mr. Belden finished speaking. The silence was broken by

Brian saying, "Thanks, Dad. I was feeling awfully angry until you said that. I'm glad you — "

Brian broke off as Mart, who was sitting closest to the radio, put his fingers to his lips and turned up the volume.

". . . further word on the explosion that occurred tonight in Sleepyside-on-the-Hudson during the Memorial Day parade," the announcer was saying.

"The blast took place at eight P.M., just as the Torchlight Parade was near its midpoint. The parade was the one hundred seventeenth annual event, and the first ever to fail to reach its natural conclusion."

"Oh, who cares about all that stuff?" Trixie said impatiently. "Just tell us where the fire was and what caused it and whether anyone was hurt!"

". . . no word yet on the cause of the explosion, which originated in the four-hundred block of West Second Street, just two blocks from the parade route. There is no word yet on whether the buildings involved in the explosion and subsequent fire were occupied.

"It is known, however, that the two buildings were a store and a warehouse, neither of which would normally be occupied in the evening.

"Efforts of fire fighters to put out the blaze were hampered by the throngs of spectators who — "

The announcer's account of the fire ceased abruptly as Mart turned the radio off. "We don't need to hear any more about the rudeness of the spectators. We got to see it for ourselves."

"It's lucky the explosion happened tonight," Honey said. "I mean, it's not lucky that the explosion *happened*, of course. And it's not lucky that all those people were on Main Street. But it *is* lucky they were on Main Street because then they couldn't be anywhere else. I mean, they couldn't be where the explosion was. You know what I mean," she concluded lamely.

"*I* know what you mean," Trixie said. "There are never any shops open in Sleepyside during the parade because there aren't any people around. Well, that is, there are lots of people around, but there aren't any people around *shopping*. Oh, woe. I know what Honey means. Now does anybody know what *I* mean?"

"I think you *both* mean that chances are nobody was hurt in the explosion or fire," Jim said. "I hope you're right. But there are bound to be some businesses hurt, and that hurts people who own them and work in them."

"Businesses!" Trixie exclaimed. "Gleeps!" She jumped up and ran out of the room, leaving a bewildered group of people watching her. Moments later she was back, the phone book open and balanced on the palm of one hand. "'Four thirty-one West Second Street,'" she read. She slammed the book shut and, with a look of despair, she said, "That's the address of Nick Roberts's father's shop!"

"Oh, no!" Honey Wheeler groaned.

3 * A Meeting of the Bob-Whites

"OH, NO!" Trixie shouted the next morning when she sat down at the breakfast table and saw the front page of the *Sleepyside Sun*.

The newspaper's headline was "Explosion Wrecks Parade." Under the headline, the entire top half of the paper was devoted to two pictures. On the left, the seven Bob-Whites smiled happily over the caption "Before." On the right, captioned "After," a milling, bewildered crowd blocked the fire truck.

Below the two pictures, a long story, written by Jane Dix-Strauss, told about the explosion and fire, and about the parade goers' interference with attempts to get to the fire.

"That's just disgusting," Trixie said. She tossed the paper facedown on the table and jabbed angrily at her cornflakes with a spoon.

Mart Belden, who was already finishing his second bowl of cereal, picked up the paper and studied it. "I assume you mean the self-centered persistence of the spectators' surveillance," he said. "I agree that it is disgusting. I appreciate the paper's admonitory function in portraying it so vividly."

"I agree," Brian Belden said, coming out of the kitchen with a plate of peanut-butter toast and a glass of milk. "I hope that the people who see themselves in that picture will think twice before they stand around to watch another fire."

"That isn't what I meant at all!" Trixie exclaimed impatiently. "You're saying all the people in that second picture should be embarrassed to be plastered all over the front page. But what about that first picture? *I* happen to think that one's pretty humiliating, too!"

Brian picked up the copy of the *Sun* and looked at the front page. "You're talking about the picture of the Bob-Whites, obviously. I get that much. But I don't know what's so humiliating about it."

"You're kidding!" Trixie exclaimed in disbelief. "It's the morning after the worst disaster in the history of Sleepyside. Your picture is on the front page of the paper, and you're grinning as though you didn't have a care in the world. You don't see anything wrong with that?"

"I *didn't* have a care in the world at the time that picture was taken," Brian said. "That, in fact, is the point of this picture. See here, where it says 'Before'? Nobody's going to think we're smiling *now*, Trixie."

"This flawed feedback seems like a febrile manifestation," Mart said.

Trixie opened her mouth to retort, then closed it and shook her head. "All right, Mart," she said. "You've got me this time. I have no idea what you just said."

"Mart means — and I think he has a good point — that you've literally worried yourself sick about Nick Roberts and his father since last night," Brian told his sister.

"Oh, Brian, you're right," Trixie said, ignoring the fact that Mart had actually made the point first. "I don't think I slept a wink last night. I suppose I did overreact to those pictures, but it just hurts to be reminded that I was so happy last night, when I'm so miserable now."

"Well," Brian said, "at the risk of making you even more miserable, I suppose I should tell you this morning's news. I heard on the radio that the site of the explosion was the Roberts Trophy Shop."

"It happened right there *in* Nick Roberts's father's store?" Trixie shrilled.

"In the basement of that store," Brian said. "The store is badly damaged, of course, and so is the warehouse next to it. But there's a lot more good news than bad news. Nobody was killed — nobody was even hurt, except for a couple of fire fighters who inhaled too much smoke. What's even more remarkable is that the fire fighters limited the damage to those two buildings, even though they were held up so badly waiting for the crowd to clear out."

"None of that good news helps Mr. Roberts," Trixie pointed out.

"In a way it does," Brian said. "I'm sure he'd feel much worse if someone had been killed trying to save his store. Anyway, worrying about it doesn't help Mr. Roberts, either. I think you'd better let go of this thing before you really do get sick."

"If ailments enthrall you, might I recommend that you contemplate the condition of the Bob-White clubhouse? Such cogitations will create that condition, I'm sure," Mart said.

"Yipes!" Trixie said, her dejected look instantly replaced by an agitated one. "I'd forgotten all about the clubhouse! Today's the day we're all supposed to meet there, to see how it got through the winter and decide what repairs it needs this summer!"

"The agreed-upon hour is ten A.M.," Mart said. "Consequently, less anxiety and more action on your part would be advisable."

"Okay," Trixie said. "I'll hurry up and get ready, but that doesn't mean I'll stop worrying about Nick and his family." Trixie tossed her napkin onto the table and hurried upstairs.

Moments later, she came back down, pulling a V-neck sweater over her plaid shirt. The sun pouring in through the windows was warm, but she knew from experience that the clubhouse would still be giving off the chill it had taken in over the winter.

"Aren't you ready *yet*?" she asked her brothers teasingly.

"We are indeed," Brian said, rising from the table and picking up his dishes. "We'll just go out through the kitchen so we can take our dishes to the sink. I'd suggest you do the same, since Moms is being good enough to let you out of spring chores this morning."

"Oh, Brian, you're right," Trixie said, hurrying

over to the table and picking up the cereal bowl and milk glass she'd left there. In the kitchen, she rinsed out her dishes in the sink, and then paused to hug her mother, who was standing at the stove. "I *do* appreciate the morning off," she said. "I'll work twice as hard this afternoon to make up for it, I promise I will."

"I know you will," Mrs. Belden said. "And since our main task today is to finish getting the seed-lings into the garden, I'd say starting first thing this afternoon is a good idea. The ground will have a few extra hours to warm up. We'll have a few extra hours without aching backs, as well!"

Trixie groaned and placed one hand on her lower back, anticipating the ache that would be there before bedtime. "Oh, woe," she said. "All those little tomatoes and beans and onions to put in all those little tiny holes in all those long, straight lines. Are you sure the garden is worth all that work?"

"Well, why don't you think about all the chili and spaghetti sauce and green beans with bacon we'll be having in a few months. Then you can tell me whether or not it's worthwhile," Helen Belden said.

"Yum!" Trixie said. "It's worth it, it's worth it! I'll be your willing slave all afternoon."

"Right now," Brian said, "what you need to be is a dedicated club member. Let's go, Trix!"

Calling final good-byes, the three Beldens left the house and walked down the path to their clubhouse.

The clubhouse, which was on the Wheeler estate, had originally been the gatehouse for the Manor House. It had fallen into disuse and been hidden by weeds for years before the Bob-Whites rediscovered it and made it their own. They had spent hours working on the two-room building, adding a wood floor over the dirt one, fixing the roof, which had caved in during a storm, and putting up shelves in the storage room for sports equipment. With the addition of the bright, cheerful curtains that Honey had sewed, the conference room of the clubhouse had become a favorite place for meetings, parties, and projects.

Because of its remote location, winters tended to be hard on the clubhouse. Each spring, the Bob-Whites had to repair the damage caused by howling winds and sub-zero temperatures. Each year, too, they tried to make a few repairs or improvements that would make the clubhouse more useful and comfortable than it had been the year before. The problem, though, was that everyone had a different idea of how the limited time and money for the clubhouse should be spent. At the spring meeting, the Bob-Whites decided whose ideas they'd turn into action.

When Trixie and her brothers entered the clubhouse, the meeting was ready to begin. Honey and Jim were already there, as were Dan and Di. Dan and Di were the least active members of the Bob-Whites. Dan's work kept him too busy for many of the activities. Di's two sets of twin brothers and sisters kept her busy as well, even though each set of twins had a private nurse. But everyone knew that this meeting was too important to pass up.

"Oh, Trixie, did you see our pictures in the paper this morning?" Di asked.

"I certainly did," Trixie said, her welcoming smile instantly turning to a scowl. "I think that—"

"Ahem," Jim said, acting quickly to head off a tirade from Trixie. "As co-president of the Bob-Whites of the Glen, I hereby call this meeting to order. Is that all right with you, Madame Co-President?"

"That's fine," Trixie said with a wave of her hand. "I'd just as soon not think about the picture or the parade or any of the rest of it, ever again."

"Thank you," Jim said. "The first and only item on today's agenda is to decide what summer projects we want to take on for the clubhouse. I suggest that we all have a little tour first, to see what damage was done this winter and remind our-selves of the projects we'd thought of last fall."

The tour didn't take long. Soon the Bob-Whites were back in their seats, all of them looking de-jected.

"All of the windowpanes need reputtying," Dan said. "The breeze is blowing right through."

"The condition of the decorative pigment is pa-thetic," Mart said.

"The paint job *is* bad," Brian said. "The worst part is that paint *isn't* just decorative. It protects the wood, too, which means we'll have even worse problems if we don't get the clubhouse painted this summer."

"At least the inside still looks nice," Trixie said, looking around at the cozy little room.

"Correction — the conference room looks nice. The storage room is a mess," Jim said. "I thought we'd built enough shelves in there to store every-thing we'd ever own, but they're already full. We'll have to add more."

"Paint, putty, and shelves," Vice-President Honey Wheeler said, writing the list down in a small notebook. "Does anyone have anything to add to the list?"

"Isn't that enough?" Trixie asked. "Painting this

whole clubhouse and puttying all those windows will take every spare moment this summer — that is, every moment I don't spend working in the garden or baby-sitting for Bobby or whatever else Moms needs help with."

"You overlook the importance of those maternal requests," Mart said. "It is through those endeavors that we will garner the funds needed to implement our plans."

"Spoken like a true treasurer," Brian told his brother. "Paint will be expensive, and the lumber for shelves won't be exactly cheap. I suppose our treasury is nearly empty, as usual."

"Unfortunately, you're right," Mart said. "Our funds might cover a small can of putty. That's about it."

"Where does it all *go?*" Trixie asked in amazement. "I work my fingers to the bone to earn my allowance, and practically every cent of it goes into the treasury. Everyone else works just as hard and gives just as much. Somehow, though, we never have any money left over in the spring. I don't understand it!"

"I think my co-president is asking for a treasurer's report, Mart," Jim said.

"Very well," Mart Belden said, taking a notebook out of his hip pocket. "Last October thirty-first, we held Halloween festivities here in the clubhouse. For said festivities we purchased two gallons of cider, cinnamon sticks, cloves, and a dozen apples for bobbing, as well as orange and black crepe paper for decorations.

"During said festivities, Ms. Wheeler reminded us of those less fortunate than ourselves, with the result that we sent a five-dollar contribution to UNICEF.

"At Christmas, we voted to buy a pair of gloves for Regan and a wool scarf for Tom Delanoy, the Wheelers' groom and chauffeur, respectively, in recognition of the help and support they had given us through the year. Bottles of cologne went to Mrs. Helen Belden and Miss Trask, Honey's governess, for the same reason.

"On February fourteenth, another festive occasion was held here at the clubhouse, for which we bought red and white crepe paper.

"In April, we voted to send ten dollars to that family near Tarrytown whose home was destroyed by a flood. That," Mart concluded, shutting the notebook, "leaves our treasury with a total of six dollars and nineteen cents as of this date."

"*Six dollars!*" Trixie shouted. "That's worse than I thought!"

"Well, I, for one, feel better," Dan said. "We did

a lot of good with the money we had, and we had a lot of fun. That's what counts."

"I agree, Dan," Brian said. "I don't think we have to feel bad about how we spent the money. We do have to worry about coming up with some more, though."

"I could ask Daddy," Honey said, without much enthusiasm.

"Oh, no, you couldn't," Trixie retorted instantly, as Honey had known one of the Bob-Whites would. "The only rules this club has are to help others and to pay our own way. If we ask for handouts, we just won't be the same club."

"I know that," Honey said. "I'd really hate asking for the money, anyway, even though I know my father would be happy to give it to us. I'm so much more proud of myself since I started earning my own spending money and club dues."

"You earn it the hard way, too," Trixie said, "repairing all of Bobby's tattered and torn clothes for Moms. Ugh! I can't stand sewing."

"Well, I *love* sewing, so earning my way isn't as horrible as you make it sound. You actually work a lot harder, gardening and chasing after Bobby and trying to keep him from making all those tatters and tears than I get paid for mending," Honey said loyally.

"Ahem," Jim said again. "That kind of mutual

admiration is what's so wonderful about the Bob-Whites, but right now we have other things to discuss. Does anyone have any ideas for raising money?"

An uncommon silence followed Jim's question. "I take it that's a *no*," Jim said, grinning in spite of himself. "Well, I'm glad we held this meeting as early in the summer as we did. We still have time to raise the money *and* get the work done. If anyone thinks of anything, let the rest of us know."

"*I* just thought of something," Honey said.

"Oh, good!" Trixie said. "What?"

"Miss Trask had Celia pack us a lunch," Honey said, whisking a picnic hamper out from under her chair.

"Oh, you!" Trixie said, giving her best friend a playful swipe.

"Once again, attention to my alimentary system will alleviate my agitation," said Mart.

"You mean the food will take our minds off our problems, just as it did last night," Trixie said. "It didn't work for me last night, though, and I don't think it will work now, since you've reminded me of it."

"Oh, no," Brian groaned. "Look what you've done, Mart. You've got Trixie worrying about Nick Roberts and his father again."

"Why are you worried, Trixie?" Di asked.

"Have you heard something more about the store?"

"Something *more*?" Trixie echoed in amazement. "How much more do you need? The store is gone, and that means Mr. Roberts is out of business."

"What makes you think that?" Jim asked, unwrapping the sandwich that Honey had just given him.

"Well, the store blew up, didn't it? How can Mr. Roberts stay in business if all his equipment and inventory and everything are gone?"

"Haven't you ever heard of something called insurance?" Jim asked. "Mr. Roberts probably had his business insured. If not, the owner of the building probably had the *building* insured. Mr. Roberts will be back in business in no time."

"Of course!" Honey said. "Oh, Trixie, isn't that wonderful! Now you can stop worrying!"

Trixie took the sandwich that Honey gave to her and smiled her thanks without speaking. Somehow, she just couldn't believe that all of the worries about Nick Roberts and his father were over.

4 * "Arson!"

"JUST THINK," Trixie said to Honey on the following afternoon as they got on the school bus. "Day after day after tomorrow, we'll be *free*, for three whole months!"

"Well, we won't have to go to school for three months," Honey said cautiously. "I don't know if I'd call that freedom, though. Unless you mean that we'll be free to spend hours working on the clubhouse and even more hours trying to figure out some way to pay for the materials."

"Oh, woe," Trixie said, slumping down in her seat. "I'd forgotten about the clubhouse problem.

Maybe I should use that, instead of the fire, to take my mind off the geometry and history tests I still have to face."

"If your grades are as bad as mine are," Honey said, "you'd better not use *anything* to take your mind off your schoolwork. If I don't study day and night between now and Friday, I'll spend the summer in summer school and be no use to the Bob-Whites."

"Your grades aren't *that* bad, Honey Wheeler," Trixie said reprovingly. It was true that Honey had once had problems with her grades, as had Trixie. But the general enthusiasm of the Bob-Whites seemed to have infected even the girls' schoolwork. Now, while they weren't exactly scholars, their grades were much better than they had been. "I didn't really mean what I said about using the fire to take my mind off my schoolwork, either. In fact, at this point I'd gladly use my schoolwork to take my mind off the fire. I'm really sick of hearing about it."

It was impossible to avoid the subject of the fire, though. It had been a major and memorable happening in the little town of Sleepyside-on-the-Hudson, and everyone wanted to talk about it.

Ka-boom! was still Bobby Belden's favorite sound. He shared his memories of the explosion with his brothers and sister time and time again. "Didja see how *red* it was when it went *ka-boom*, Trixie?" he'd ask. "Didja hear how *loud* it was?"

Trixie would answer, "I saw it, Bobby, and I heard it. It wasn't fun, though, it was awful — really awful. Two buildings were destroyed and it's just a miracle that nobody was hurt. Do you understand that?"

In response to his sister's question, Bobby always nodded solemnly and said, "It was really awful, Trixie." But moments later he'd be enthusiastically yelling "*Ka-boom!*" again.

"He's just too young to understand," Brian had said quietly after one of Bobby's *ka-boom*s had made Trixie jump in fright. "Don't worry, though, tomorrow something new will catch his attention and he'll forget all about the fire."

"I hope we can all start to forget," Trixie had told her brother.

Trixie's hope wasn't to be realized. On Saturday morning when she came downstairs to breakfast, the school year was part of the past, but the fire seemed destined more than ever to be part of the town's future.

"Arson!" screamed the headline on the front page of the *Sleepyside Sun*. Brian and Mart were already huddled over the paper when Trixie joined them at the table.

"Gleeps!" Trixie exclaimed when she saw the big, black type. "Do they really think the fire was set deliberately?"

"The authorities are no longer speculating," Mart said. "The cogency of the evidence is beyond contradiction."

"They know it's arson?" Trixie guessed from Mart's windy description.

"That's right," Brian said. "The fire marshal says that the fire was deliberately set in the basement of Mr. Roberts's store."

"The alligation permits the authorities to make that allegation," Mart said.

"What's he talking about?" Trixie asked in near desperation, turning back to Brian.

"Alligation is the word the fire experts use for deep crimp marks, like alligator skin. They show up on wood at the point of origin — the place where the fire's been set. Any natural fire would have only one point of origin. But in the basement of Mr. Roberts's store, the investigators found *six* points of origin. That, in itself, is almost a sure sign of arson," Brian said.

"How can they possibly know that?" Trixie asked. "How can they find the points of origin of a fire that's burned a whole building to a crisp?"

"That's just the thing," Brian said. "The building wasn't burned to a crisp, although it should have been."

"The arsonist's plan failed," Mart added.

"How could it have gone wrong?" Trixie asked. "If you start a fire in six different places, it seems to me that it's going to *burn*. It *did* burn. We saw it!"

"Correction," Brian said. "We saw it *explode*. That's what went wrong. Apparently the arsonist poured a lot of flammable liquid, like gasoline, in six different places. If he'd then started the fire immediately, there would have been such total destruction from the fire that it would have been impossible to determine anything. Instead, he must have taken his time, and while he was taking his time, the liquid was evaporating, and the vapors were rising to the ceiling. When the arsonist finally lit the fire, there wasn't much liquid to burn — but there was a lot of vapor to explode. That's how we wound up with the big *ka-boom* and the traces of arson left behind."

"That's fascinating!" Trixie said. "I had no idea the fire investigators could prove so much."

"Unfortunately, these specialists have ample opportunity to practice their profession," Mart said. "The statistics in this sidebar are staggering. One source quoted here states that arson may cost as much as one *billion* dollars a year."

"One *billion*? With a *b*?" Trixie asked. "As in a one followed by nine zeros?"

"My sibling has a clearer concept of numerals than I had previously supposed," Mart said.

"One billion it is," Brian told her. "I read that sidebar, too. Another source quoted says that almost forty percent of the fires that occur in this country are set deliberately."

"But *why*?" Trixie demanded. "Why would anyone want to destroy property and risk lives? Even if the buildings are insured, it's stupid to burn them down."

"The perceived wisdom lies precisely in the protection afforded by insurance," Mart said, "as you must surely realize if you ponder your prattle for a moment."

"Oh," Trixie said, realizing that her statement had sounded very silly. "You mean that people would set their buildings on fire to claim the insurance on them."

"That's one of the biggest reasons for arson," Brian said. "Sometimes people over-insure a rundown building and burn it so that they get more money than they could by selling it. Sometimes people want to keep the building but remodel it. Setting a small fire in the room they want to remodel is a good way of raising the money, they think."

"Not all arsonists have monetary aspirations," Mart added. "Vengeance is a motivator, as well."

Trixie shuddered. "Can you imagine hating someone so much that you'd burn down his house or his store to get even with him?"

"I can't imagine it," Brian admitted. "But according to the article, people do it. Or they hire professionals to do it for them. There's a third reason for arson, too. In spite of what Dad said the other night, some people really do love to set fires and watch them burn."

"Ugh!" Trixie said, shuddering again and wrinkling her nose in disgust. "That's even worse than setting a fire for revenge! Don't tell me any more. I think I've heard as much about arson as I want to know!"

"The coverage was admirably complete," Mart said, with a wink at his brother that Trixie didn't see.

"I thought so," Brian said. "Don't you agree, Trixie? You may not like all the information we just gave you, but you have to admit it's pretty complete on such short notice."

"That is true, I suppose," Trixie said absentmindedly, her attention already on the comic strips.

"Yes," Brian continued casually, "I knew you'd agree that Jane Dix-Strauss did a first-rate job."

Trixie's head jerked up so fast that her curls had to hurry to catch up. "Jane Dix-Strauss! Is that where you got all that stuff?" She grabbed the front page out of Mart's hands and looked at the article on arson. Sure enough, the young reporter's name was prominently displayed above the story. "Ugh!" With an expression of distaste, she shoved the paper back at her "almost twin" brother.

"But, Trixie, you said you thought the coverage was excellent!" Brian said in mock-innocence.

"You tricked me into saying the story was good," Trixie retorted. "Before that, what I said on my own was that I didn't want to hear another word about arson. I don't understand why Jane Dix-Strauss keeps writing all those depressing news articles. Does she just enjoy spoiling people's breakfasts?"

The teasing smile faded from Brian's face, and he told his sister seriously, "You don't know that Jane Dix-Strauss enjoys writing about fires, Trix. She may hate them as much as you do — worse, even. But as a top-notch reporter, she has to give the facts."

"'Top-notch' doesn't have to be rude," Trixie retorted.

Just then the phone started to ring, and Trixie, relieved at the interruption, jumped up to answer it.

All thoughts of Jane Dix-Strauss were pushed out of her mind when she recognized the distraught voice of Nick Roberts.

"They've arrested my father!" he told her.

5 * A Trip to Jail

"Arrested!" Trixie's voice was barely a squeak. "Why? When?"

"They just came and took him away a few min-utes ago. They say they want to talk to him about the fire." Nick's voice was strained. He was just barely managing to keep himself under control.

"Oh, Nick, that's awful! They can't do that! Your father didn't do it! Is there something we can do?" Trixie knew she was rattling on confusedly, but she couldn't express her tangled thoughts any more clearly.

"I need the name of an attorney," Nick said.

"Of course, you do," Trixie agreed. "Dad has already left for the bank, but I'll call him and ask him whom he can recommend. Then I'll call you right back." She pushed down the button to disconnect Nick, released it, and started to dial the bank.

"What's going on?"

Trixie was so lost in her concern for Nick Roberts and his father that the voice sounding close behind her made her jump and whirl around. Both of her brothers were standing there.

"It was Nick," Trixie told them. "The police have arrested his father. They think he set fire to his own store!"

"An abhorrently asinine accusation!" Mart exclaimed angrily.

Brian winced and shook his head. "I didn't even want to say it out loud, but given the location of the fire and Mr. Roberts's previous dealings with criminals, I really was afraid he might be a suspect."

"But Nick's father is innocent!" Trixie said.

"I agree with you. But obviously the police aren't so sure. Why did Nick call here?" Brian asked.

"Gleeps!" Trixie exclaimed, suddenly remembering the telephone receiver in her hand and the all-important call she still hadn't made. "Nick needs a lawyer. I'm to call Dad and ask for the name of one," she explained while she dialed.

"I know just the right person," Mr. Belden said when Trixie had breathlessly explained the problem. "Pat Murphy, a fine attorney who's interested in justice *and* the law. I'll call and see if Pat's free. You wait by the phone."

Trixie hung up and relayed her father's message to her brothers. All three of the Beldens stared at the phone through a silence that seemed to stretch on forever. When the ring finally did shatter the stillness, all three of them jumped.

"Dad?" Trixie asked when she picked up the phone.

"Pat Murphy is headed over to the jail now. Pat knows the background of the case, of course — everyone in Sleepyside does. The first concern is to find out whether Mr. Roberts has been, or is going to be, charged. Then Pat will see about arranging bail. Do you want to tell Nick?"

"I certainly do," Trixie said warmly. "Thanks, Dad. You're perfectly perfect!"

Trixie dialed Nick Roberts's number. "There's an attorney going over to talk to your father right now," she told Nick when he answered on the second ring. "Pat Murphy—one of the best, Dad says."

"Thank you," Nick said. He sounded dazed. "I

guess I'll — I think — Dad said to wait here with Mother, but I can't. I'm going over to the jail, too. Mother will be much more relieved to know I'm doing what I can for Dad."

"I think that's a good idea," Trixie told him. "Why don't you let us come pick you up in Brian's car?" Realizing that she had just committed Brian's car and both her brothers' time, she turned to look at them. Her brothers both nodded emphatically before she could even ask the question. "See you in a minute," she added, putting down the receiver before Nick could protest.

It was, indeed, only a matter of minutes before the three Beldens were in the car, headed for Nick Roberts's house. In those minutes there had been hurried explanations to their mother and a pulling on of jackets because of the threat of rain. Trixie wished that there had also been time for a call to the Manor House. In a situation like this, she wanted Honey and Jim nearby. Trixie wasn't the one in need, though; Nick Roberts was, and his needs had to be put first. She decided she would try to call Honey and Jim from the police station.

As soon as Brian pulled into Nick's drive, Trixie jumped out of the car, walked quickly up to the front door, and rang the bell. Nick opened the door almost immediately. He looked haggard and pale.

"I'll just tell Mother I'm leaving," he said softly.

He disappeared into the back of the house and Trixie stood waiting. The house was so unnaturally quiet that she felt goosebumps rising on her arms. Although there were three human beings in this house, the life seemed to have gone out of it. When Nick returned, Trixie led the way quickly back outside.

It didn't take long to get to the police station. Nick found the receptionist and asked her, "Can I see my father? His name is Nicholas Roberts."

"I'm sorry," the receptionist said, not sounding sorry at all. "Your father is speaking with his attorney at the moment. You can go see him when Pat Murphy is finished."

Nick nodded his acceptance of this cold fact and led his friends to a row of uncomfortable-looking molded-plastic chairs that sat along one wall.

There was a long period of silence. Then Brian asked, "How did this happen, Nick? Do you know why your father is a suspect?"

Nick seemed to come slowly back from some great distance away. "The first idea we had that my father might be a suspect came last night," he said. "That's when we got a phone call from Mr. Slettom. He was our landlord at the store. He owned both of the buildings that burned, in fact.

Mr. Slettom said that the police had been questioning him. He said he realized he'd given answers that made things look bad for my father, but he couldn't help it. He was just telling the truth. That's why he called, to apologize."

"What kinds of questions did the police ask Mr. Slettom?" Brian asked.

"They wanted to know how long my father had been renting the space in his building. Then they wanted to know whether my father had a long-term lease. When Mr. Slettom said he did, they asked if my father had ever indicated he'd like to get out of the lease. Mr. Slettom had to tell them that my father had asked just a couple of months ago if the lease could be broken. Business had gotten a lot better lately, you see, and we really needed more room and wanted a better location.

"Mr. Slettom had told my father that he'd try to rent the space, but he couldn't find any takers. It's cheap to rent, but that's about all you can say for it. Mr. Slettom had to tell the police all that, of course. Not about the cheap rent — the rest of it, I mean."

"That's a slender thread on which to hang a suspicion of arson," Mart said.

"There was also the fact of my father's previous dealings with shady characters," Nick continued.

"My father didn't report those criminals who tried to get him to work for them. The police have never understood that Dad was afraid to turn them in because they'd threatened to harm my mother. I think those old suspicions, plus Mr. Slettom's testimony, are what made the police decide to question Dad.

"One of the questions they asked was where my father was at the time of the explosion. Dad told them that when the explosion occurred, he was with Mother and me on Main Street, watching the parade. But he also had to admit that he'd been working at the store up until a few minutes before the parade started."

"I remember that," Trixie said. "I mean, I remember seeing him join you and your mother just before the start of the parade. We remarked about how nice it was that your father was so busy these days —" Trixie broke off as she realized how painful that reminder of happier times must be for her friend.

Nick didn't seem to look any sadder after Trixie's comment, though. Maybe it was impossible for him to get any sadder than he already was. Instead, he just nodded and continued. "The police say it would have been easy for Dad to have set the fire with a fuse so he'd be on Main Street when it started. That would explain how the fuel had time to evaporate. They also say it would have been impossible for Dad not to have heard the *real* arsonist moving around in the basement, if Dad was really upstairs working when he said he was."

"Does your father remember hearing any suspicious noises?" Brian asked.

Nick shook his head. "As I told you, it's a pretty rundown building. There are always lots of noises — wind blowing through cracks, things creaking and popping. Even mice scurrying around. You get so you don't hear any of the noises; if you did, it would be too creepy to stay there at all."

"Gleeps," Trixie said. "I can see why your father wanted out of his lease." Realizing that she'd once again said the worst possible thing, she clapped her hand over her mouth. "Oh, Nick, I didn't mean — I mean —"

"I know what you meant," Nick said with what seemed to be a genuine smile. "You're right. We did want out of that lease. Not *that* badly, though."

"Couldn't Mr. Slettom have done something about the drafts and the mice, so that you wouldn't want to break your lease?" Brian asked.

"No amount of repairs would have helped with the lack of space," Nick pointed out. "Besides, fixing up that building would just have given Mr.

Slettom a good building in a bad neighborhood. I doubt that he'd have been able to raise the rent enough to cover the cost of the repairs. I agree that Mr. Slettom's building isn't very attractive, but we were grateful to get it for the price when we first moved here."

Nobody responded to Nick's logical defense of Mr. Slettom. There didn't seem to be anything more to say. A deathly silence fell on the little group once again. Trixie suddenly remembered that she hadn't called Honey and Jim. She began to look around for a pay telephone.

Her search was interrupted by loud voices coming from down the hall. Trixie looked in the direction of the noise and saw Sergeant Molinson walking toward them. He was being pursued by an attractive, middle-aged woman who was wearing a tweed suit and carrying a bulging briefcase.

"This is absurd!" the woman shouted. "There is absolutely no justice in holding that poor man when you haven't a shred of a case against him!"

Remembering what her father had said about sending Mr. Roberts an attorney who understood justice as well as law, Trixie whispered, "That must be Pat Murphy."

Brian nodded, but he kept his eyes on the woman who was standing next to the sergeant.

"There are only two ways of proving arson. You can catch the perpetrator in the act or you can show exclusive opportunity. Neither of those rules applies here."

"He had motive —" Sergeant Molinson began belligerently.

"Motive doesn't count!" Pat Murphy snapped. "Can you show intent?"

Sergeant Molinson didn't reply, but the red flush that spread across his jowly face provided the answer.

"I'll tell you why you arrested Nicholas Roberts," the attorney continued. "It wasn't because of motive. It was because of media." Without warning, Pat Murphy turned and thrust out an accusing finger.

Looking in the direction in which the lawyer had pointed, Trixie was shocked to see Jane Dix-Strauss standing in the corridor, note pad in hand. At first, Trixie didn't understand Pat Murphy's statement. Then, suddenly, she realized what it meant. *The police would never have arrested Mr. Roberts on such flimsy evidence if it hadn't been for that article about arson*, Trixie thought. *They might have suspected him. They might even have questioned him. But they wouldn't have put him in jail if Jane Dix-Strauss hadn't written that ar-*

ticle. It's her fault Mr. Roberts is behind bars!

All eyes had turned toward Jane Dix-Strauss, and Trixie was delighted to see how uncomfortable she looked. Then everyone's attention turned back to Pat Murphy as the attorney once again began to speak. "That journalist wrote a report of the fire that was more inflammatory than the fire itself. She dug up a bunch of facts and figures that made it sound as though all of Sleepyside is about to go up in flames. With her getting the populace all riled up, you chose the easiest way to get them calmed down — and that was to arrest an innocent man!"

"I don't let a hotshot reporter buffalo me!" Sergeant Molinson growled.

"Prove it!" Pat Murphy said. "Release Nicholas Roberts!"

"And you don't buffalo me, either," Molinson snapped. "I can hold Roberts for forty-eight hours for questioning without pressing charges. And that's what I intend to do!" With that, the sergeant walked quickly out of the room.

6 * At the Scene of the Crime

AFTER SERGEANT MOLINSON LEFT, Pat Murphy turned and saw the four young people for the first time. Her look of stony determination melted into a warm and genuine smile as she walked toward them. "Nick?" she asked, holding out her hand to the young artist. "It had to be you — you look like your father."

"How is my father?" Nick asked.

"I won't say he's fine, because nobody would be under the circumstances," Pat Murphy told him. "He's doing as well as can be expected. You can go in and see him, if you'd like."

"I will," Nick said. "When do you think he'll be released?"

Pat Murphy looked at the floor and flapped her briefcase impatiently against her leg. "He should have been released already, and you probably have me to blame for the fact that he hasn't been. I shouldn't have lost my temper. It just made Molinson dig in his heels. My guess is that he'll hold your father for a few hours, to save face, and then let him go. If he isn't home by tomorrow morning, give me a call."

"I'll do that," Nick said. "And please, don't think it's your fault that they're holding my father here. They probably would have done that anyway."

"I hope you're right," Pat Murphy said. "Well, if you want to stop in and visit your father, just go through those double doors back there. The clerk will take you to him. Only family and legal counsel allowed, I'm afraid," she added, turning to the Beldens.

"I should have introduced you," Nick said apologetically. "This is Trixie, Mart, and Brian Belden. Their father was the one who called you."

"Pleased to meet you," Pat Murphy said. "Your father is a good man."

"He says the same thing about you," Trixie told the lawyer. "I mean — that is —" She felt the dreaded blush creeping up her neck.

"I know what you mean," Pat Murphy said, laughing.

Trixie smiled at the attorney.

"I really have to be going," Pat Murphy said. "Nick, I'll be talking to you later." She put out her hand again, and Nick shook it gratefully.

The attorney walked briskly toward the door — only to be stopped by Jane Dix-Strauss, who approached her with note pad in hand. Pat Murphy drew herself up to her full height and glared at the young reporter. "I have no comment to make to you," she snapped. "What's more, it will be a cold day in June before I *do* have one." She pushed past the reporter and made her way out the door.

"Wow!" Trixie breathed. "I guess *she* told *her*."

"Your statement is correct," Mart told her. "Nevertheless, the journalist seems unjarred by the barrister's barrage."

"Cool as a cucumber," Brian agreed. "Uh-oh — I think she's thinking of heading this way. Nick, you'd better go in to see your father. We'll run some errands and meet you back here in an hour."

Outside, the sky was cloudy and the air was cool for the first week in June. But the weather wasn't the only reason for Trixie's shiver as she got into the car. "Can you imagine having to go visit your father in *jail*?" she asked. "I don't think I could bring myself to do it. Poor Nick — and he's so calm about it."

"I don't think he's calm at all," Brian said. "He's just quiet. I bet there's plenty of hurt under the surface. I worry more about people like that than I do about the ones who let go and show they're upset."

"Speaking of letting go," Trixie said, "where are we going now? What are the errands we have to run for an hour?"

"I thought we'd go to the lumberyard and price the supplies we'll need for the clubhouse," Brian said as he turned out of the parking lot.

"The only activity less fun than staying at the jail," Mart said with a sigh.

"I'll grant you it will be depressing to find out how much the repairs will cost," Brian admitted. "But we have to start somewhere."

"How could this place be depressing?" Trixie asked a few minutes later as she led the way into the lumberyard. "That wonderful smell of sawdust always makes me happy. And there's so much to see."

"Let's start with the shelving," said Brian, always businesslike. "Should we use real oak shelving like this or get pine one-by-tens the way we did before?"

"One-by-tens, of course," Trixie said. "We'll never be able to afford real oak. It's beautiful, though."

"Right you are," Brian said. "The pine boards are back this way."

The lumber was disappointing after the beautiful, fine-grained oak they'd just looked at. The price, although lower, was still astounding when Brian added it all up.

"At least we know," he said. "Let's move on to the paint."

"Look at all these beautiful colors," Trixie said, waving her hand at the sample swatches that were hung on the walls of the paint department. "Do we have to paint the clubhouse white again? I know white is a nice, practical color. It's just that some of these others are so attractive."

"Well, take a sample card," Brian said. "I think we have to stick to white for the clubhouse, but not for the trim. Another color might really add some zip if we used it for the window frames and the door."

"Oh, that's a wonderful idea!" Trixie's eyes gleamed, and she quickly took a color swatch card and put it in her pocket. "We can have a special meeting of the Bob-Whites to choose a color."

"We can also tell them how much the paint will cost," Brian said, working out the final figure on his scrap of paper.

"How much?" Trixie asked.

"Too much," Brian said, putting the paper in his pocket. "Let's check the putty. That's something I know we can afford."

"I figured we'd be able to do some shopping this morning," Mart said. "So I brought along our club's assets, such as they are."

"Good thinking," Brian told him. "We might as well buy some putty while we're here. That's one project we can get going on right away."

The Beldens made their small purchase with a feeling of accomplishment. "Summer is officially here," Trixie said, "since the repairs to the clubhouse have officially begun."

Outside, though, it was harder to believe that summer was on its way. A cold spring rain had started to fall.

It's too bad it wasn't raining during the Memorial Day parade, Trixie thought. *Then the fire couldn't have done as much damage. Maybe it wouldn't have spread to the warehouse at all.* That thought reminded Trixie of something else.

She grabbed Brian's arm as he started up the car. "Do we have any time left before we're to meet Nick?" she asked.

"A few minutes," Brian told her. "Why?"

"We haven't seen Mr. Roberts's store since the fire. Let's drive past it now."

"All right," Brian said. "There probably won't be much to see, though."

When they arrived at Mr. Roberts's former store a few minutes later, Trixie couldn't help but feel disappointed that her brother's prediction had been so accurate. Plywood had replaced the windows and the glass in the door. The brick building itself showed few signs of damage other than some darkening around the window frames. Only some debris that still remained along the sidewalk and the sparkle of tiny bits of broken glass gave a hint as to what had happened there.

"Do you suppose we could look around?" Trixie asked.

"I suppose *we* could, but *we* don't want to. Some of us, anyway, want to stay in the car where it's warm and dry," Brian said.

"An admirable observation," Mart agreed.

"Well, would you wait here while *I* look around?" Trixie asked.

"Oh, Trixie," Brian said with a sigh. "All right.

Be careful, though. Don't trip on a loose brick or cut yourself on broken glass. Don't be too long, either — we don't want to keep Nick waiting."

"I'll be right back," Trixie said. She jumped out of the car and, turning up the collar of her jacket, walked along the side of the building. Away from the sidewalk, the rubble lay more thickly. There was, Trixie had to admit to herself, something eerie about the little building. Mostly, it was too quiet, the way Nick's house had been too quiet that morning.

Trixie went around the corner to the alley. From the back the damage was more noticeable. Or maybe the back of the building looked worse because so much litter and garbage were mixed in with the rubble from the fire. Trixie kicked at a brick with the toe of her shoe.

A glint of metal caught her eye. She bent down and picked up the small object that had been hidden under the brick. It was a gold button, the kind with a raised monogram on it. "JSD," Trixie read the letters aloud. "Well, Mr. JSD, you must have a fancy sports coat that's as ragged-looking as my Bob-Whites jacket." Absentmindedly, she put the button in the pocket of her jacket and continued on around the building. Minutes later, she was back in the car with her brothers.

"Well?" Brian asked. "Did you satisfy your curiosity?"

Trixie shook her head. "It wasn't really curiosity. It was more — I don't know. I guess I thought it would make more sense if I saw the building. It didn't work, though. It seemed too little and too shabby to cause so much trouble."

Brian patted his sister on the arm sympathetically. "Some things don't make much sense. They just take some getting used to. Now, let's go pick up Nick."

Nick was waiting under the eaves of the police station, his shoulders hunched against the rain. Brian honked as they approached, and Nick ran for the car and jumped into the back seat.

"You didn't have to wait outside for us," Trixie chided him. "We would have come in for you."

"That isn't why I waited outside," Nick said. "Jane Dix-Strauss was still lurking in the hallway when I finished talking to my father. I didn't want to deal with her, so I walked out. I hoped she'd think I'd kept on going."

"That woman!" Trixie growled.

"How's your father, Nick?" Brian asked, averting any further complaints from his sister about the *Sleepyside Sun*'s newest reporter.

"He's worried, of course," Nick said. "More

worried about Mother and me than about himself.
I tried to tell him we'd be okay. He was glad you
helped us find Pat Murphy. He liked her a lot."

"I did, too," Trixie said.

As Brian pulled out of the parking lot, his car
was nearly sideswiped by another car that was
pulling in. Brian slammed on the brakes just in
time to avoid an accident. The other car stopped,
too. The driver's door opened and a short, pudgy
man barreled out.

"Oh, woe," Trixie said. "I suppose he's going to
rant about teenage drivers, when he's the one who
almost caused the accident."

But it was to the back window of the car, not the
front, that the man directed his attention.

"It's Mr. Slettom!" Nick exclaimed. He rolled
down the window, and the little man stuck his
head inside.

Trixie turned in the seat, craning her neck to see
the man whose two buildings had just burned. It
was almost impossible to concentrate on what Mr.
Slettom looked like, because the loud, red-and-
green-plaid sports coat he wore was so over-
powering. Once she got past the garish jacket,
though, Trixie decided that the wearer was a very
uninteresting-looking man. His round face looked
even rounder because he was almost entirely
bald, with just a fringe of pale blond hair that

ringed the back of his head. He looked worried.

"I just heard about your father, Nick," he said breathlessly. "I came as soon as I could. Is he all right? Is there anything I can do? Do you need bail money?"

Nick held up one hand to stop the flow of questions. "Thank you, Mr. Slettom. I really appreciate your offering to help. There's nothing we need, though. We have a good attorney. We can't use bail money because Dad hasn't been charged, so he can't be released on bail."

"He hasn't been charged? How dare they hold him that way! Still, I suppose it's for the best — I mean, if they *don't* charge him, it will be better for his record in the long run.

"Oh, Nick, I'm just so sorry," Mr. Slettom continued. "I really feel as though it's all my fault, because I told the police about your father's wanting out of his lease. Are you sure there's nothing more I can do?"

Nick shook his head. "I'll let you know if there is anything, though, I promise."

"Thank you, Nick. Thank you." Mr. Slettom walked back to his car, got in, and drove away.

"He certainly seems convinced of his own guilt," Mart said as they once again pulled out of the parking lot.

"Well, wouldn't you have a guilty conscience if

you'd said something that led to somebody's getting arrested?" Trixie asked.

"I would," Brian said. "It must be a helpless feeling to know you have to tell the truth, even though someone's going to be hurt by it."

"He could just as easily be angry, since the fire in the store spread to his appliance warehouse," Nick said. "He's a nice man, though. He's been very kind to us since we've been renting the shop from him. I should say, 'While we were renting the shop from him.' I can't get used to the fact that it's gone." Nick's brown eyes darkened as if the full truth of his circumstances had, in fact, just begun to sink in.

"Everything will be all right, Nick," Trixie said. "You'll see. Your father will have a bigger and better store before very long."

"I hope you're right, Trixie," Nick said as the car pulled into his driveway. He tugged at the door handle, opened the door, and climbed out. "Thanks for everything."

"No problem," Brian said as he put the car into reverse. "Keep in touch, you hear?"

Nick nodded and walked into the house.

"It certainly is mysterious, isn't it?" Trixie mused aloud.

"Aha!" Mart shouted. "The eventuality I had

anticipated has at last arrived! Our sibling shamus has surfaced once again!"

"Oh, Mart," Trixie said, "I don't mean detective-type mysterious. I mean — well, mysterious-type mysterious. The way people behave. Nick seemed unfriendly when I first met him, but he's really a warm, caring person. Mr. Slettom, who has every right to be suspicious and angry at Mr. Roberts, is actually sympathetic and eager to help. Pat Murphy, who's probably spent more time around criminals than most *criminals* have, is also a nice, warm person. And then, on the other hand —"

"There's an anti-reporter diatribe coming," Brian interrupted. "I can feel it!"

"Well, that reporter deserves one," Trixie said.

"There was a brazen aspect in Jane Dix-Strauss's attempt to interview Pat Murphy," Mart agreed.

"Being thick-skinned is part of her job," Brian said. "If she were being that persistent in trying to interview some crooked politician, we'd love it. The only difference between that and this is that someone we know is involved. Otherwise, it's the same — a reporter doing a thorough job of reporting."

"I hope she is as competent in writing about Mr.

Roberts's release from jail," Mart said.

"I hope so, too," Brian told him. "But I won't hold my breath. Arresting a suspected arsonist is of interest to everyone in Sleepyside, so it makes the front page. Releasing an innocent man is really of interest only to his friends and family, so that usually gets hidden in the back. It isn't news."

"There's one way to make Mr. Roberts's release newsworthy," Trixie said.

"Uh-oh," Brian said.

"Well, it's true," Trixie said defensively. "If Mr. Roberts is released because the *real* arsonist is caught, that will be news — just like you said."

"I follow your logic, Trix," Brian said. "But I can also take it a step farther and see you deciding to catch the arsonist yourself. I don't want you even to think about doing that. It's too dangerous. You'd be literally playing with fire!"

"Did you hear me say I was going to try to catch the arsonist? Did you?" Trixie demanded.

"No," Brian admitted. "But I do want to hear you say you won't try. Promise me, Trixie."

"I promise," Trixie said reluctantly. To herself, she added, *But that won't stop me from trying to figure out who it is.*

7 * Trixie Has a Plan

As the car headed down Glen Road, Trixie once again reached out to touch her oldest brother's arm. "Brian, would you drop me off at the Manor House? I know it's a little bit out of your way, but you can drive it faster than I can walk it, and I have to talk to Honey about all that's happened."

"There is never a dearth of detours with Beatrix directing," Mart said.

"That's okay," Brian said. "I said earlier that getting things out of your system is best. I'm sure that's what Trixie has in mind."

A few minutes later, Trixie was hopping out of

the car in front of the Manor House. "Thanks, Brian," she said. "Tell Moms I'll be home *soonest* to do my chores. I promise!" She ran up the wide steps and knocked on the front door.

Celia let her in and told her that Honey was in the den. Trixie shouted another "Thanks!" and went to find her best friend.

"Nick Roberts's father has been arrested," Trixie said as she burst in on Honey. "Mart and Brian and I just came from the police station."

"Arrested!" Honey let her sewing project drop to her lap. "Oh, Trixie, no! Can they do that?"

"They did it," Trixie said grimly. Briefly, she told Honey about the phone call from Nick, the conversation with Pat Murphy, and the intrusiveness of Jane Dix-Strauss. "Pat Murphy handled her beautifully, but Nick was so afraid of talking to her that he waited for us out in the rain. Poor guy — if I'd known, I never would have wasted time visiting his father's store."

"You visited the store?" Honey asked. "I thought it had burned down."

"It did. Well, it didn't burn down exactly. It sort of burned *out*. The windows and doors are all boarded over, and the alley is filled with rubble. There's not much to see, really. Oh — except I did find this." Trixie reached into her pocket, took out the button, and tossed it at Honey, who caught it handily.

"JDS," Honey read.

"Huh-uh, it's JSD," Trixie corrected her.

"No, it isn't, Trixie. In a monogram, the last initial goes in the middle, in a larger size, and the first two initials go on either side. So the monogram on this button says, 'JDS.'"

"Jane Dix-Strauss!" Trixie exclaimed. "I'll bet this button belongs to her."

"Those are her initials," Honey agreed. "They're probably a lot of other people's, though."

"She has a blazer with gold buttons about this size. She was wearing it the night of the fire. I wasn't close enough to see if there was a monogram, but — Oh, my gosh!" Trixie's eyes widened. "Jane Dix-Strauss was wearing a blazer with gold buttons the night of the fire. I found this gold button with her initials on it at the *scene* of the fire! Honey, do you remember whether she was missing any buttons when she talked to us on Main Street?"

"I didn't notice. In fact, I didn't even notice the gold buttons. I'm not as observant as you are — even if I am a lot more interested in clothes. But, Trixie, you can't possibly think Jane Dix-Strauss started that fire! She wouldn't have any reason to.

Besides, you just said she was *on* Main Street when the fire started. So she couldn't have been in a store *off* Main Street at the same time."

"Mr. Roberts has been arrested for starting that fire, and we saw him before we saw her," Trixie pointed out.

"All right. She could have started the fire. But why would she?" Honey asked. "If this is her button, I'm sure she lost it at the scene of the fire doing the same thing you were — investigating." She held the button out to Trixie.

"I suppose so," Trixie admitted, taking the button and dropping it back into her pocket. "I know Brian and Mart would say she's only doing her job, but she doesn't seem to care who she hurts while she's doing it. Well, I can't talk any more right now. I promised Moms I'd get tons of work done today, and the morning's already gone. Can we meet at the clubhouse tonight? All the Bob-Whites, I mean? We priced the materials for the summer repairs today, and we need to talk about what to do next."

"I don't have anything planned," Honey said. "I'm sure Jim doesn't, either. We'll check with Miss Trask and let you know."

"Super," Trixie said. "Would you call Dan and Di, too? I'll be in charge of the snacks, since you brought them last time."

With that agreed to, the girls said good-bye. Back home, Trixie quickly told her brothers about the meeting and got their mother's permission to go. Then she pitched into work. First on the agenda was the garden, where seemingly millions of tiny weeds had poked through the earth since the previous week. Tiny as they were, they had to be pulled, since the plants in the garden were even tinier.

After the garden was weeded, Trixie scrubbed as much of the dirt from her hands as she could, ate a quick lunch, then took the dust rags into the living room.

As always, she paused to admire the painting her mother had done years before, of a tree-lined stream in winter. Now she paused, too, before the pen-and-ink drawing of Crabapple Farm that she had bought from Nick Roberts at the art fair. The simple black frame set it off perfectly — *which is lucky*, Trixie thought, *since that's all I could afford.* She marveled again at Nick's talent and resolved to do everything she could to see that that talent wasn't swamped by a sea of troubles.

With the dusting done, Trixie washed the floor of the big country kitchen until it shone. Then she straightened her room and took down a load of dry clothes from the line.

Finally it was time for supper. Mart found that

night an appetite to rival his own. "To what do we owe this gust of gustatory vehemence?" he asked.

"I'm hungry because I've been working hard," Trixie said. "You ought to try it sometime. On second thought, you'd better not — the way you eat already, we couldn't afford to fill you up if you did a lot of work."

"Our day's accomplishments may not seem like much compared to yours," Brian said, "but we weren't exactly lounging around. We got the garage cleaned out, the basement straightened up, and the driveway edged."

"I'm proud of all of you," Mrs. Belden said.

"What about me, Moms?" Bobby said. "Are you proud of me?"

"Of course," Helen Belden told her youngest son. "I think I have the four best children in the whole world."

"I think they have the best mother," Peter Belden said. "Certainly they have the mother who makes the best fried chicken and" — he raised his eyebrows in hopeful questioning — "apple pie?"

"That was *supposed* to be a surprise," Mrs. Belden said in mock-despair. "It's impossible to keep a secret in this family."

"It's impossible to keep a secret that smells as good as that one," her husband agreed.

"Well, your guess was right, anyway," Mrs. Belden said. "I decided to celebrate the coming of summer by baking the last of the apple pies I froze last fall. From now on, we'll have to rely on fresh produce exclusively!"

"Yummy yum!" Trixie said. "I might feel sad about the last of the apple pies if I didn't feel so happy about the strawberry shortcake and blueberry cobbler and cherry pie that are coming!"

"Let us divest ourselves of the vestiges of the entree so that we might progress to the pastry," Mart said, rising and beginning to clear the table.

"We have to progress to the clubhouse pretty soon," Trixie said. "There will be just enough time to have dessert and do the dishes."

In the end, though, it was Mart and Brian Belden who did the dishes, because Trixie was called to the phone just as she finished the last bite of pie.

"Trixie, this is Nick Roberts," the solemn voice said. "I just wanted you to know that my father is home. Sergeant Molinson released him without pressing charges — although he made it clear that Dad isn't really off the hook yet."

"Oh, Nick, I'm so glad. About your father's being released, not about his not being off the hook," Trixie told him. "I bet he's glad to be home."

"Well," Nick said slowly, "actually, he doesn't seem glad about much of anything. He's really acting as if it's all over — as if he'll never be able to get his life back together again."

"Oh, Nick, that isn't true," Trixie protested. "I know this whole thing is awful, but it can't last forever."

"I know that," Nick said. "I told Dad we should just keep moving ahead. The insurance company is holding off on paying our claim, of course. But we have lots of inventory in the basement of our house — I told you the store was too small to hold everything. It's all paid for, and we have enough in savings to buy new equipment. We could rent a new store or work out of the house." Nick's voice had gathered enthusiasm as he spoke. The enthusiasm left suddenly, though, as he added, "Dad won't even talk about the idea. He just doesn't seem to have the energy to start over."

There was a long silence. Trixie couldn't think of any way to respond.

"Well," Nick said, "I shouldn't be bothering you with all this. I really only called to tell you that Dad is home, and to thank you for your help this morning."

"Oh, Nick, you mustn't think you were bothering me," Trixie said emphatically, realizing that her silence had been misinterpreted. "*I'm* bothering me, because I can't seem to think of anything to do about all this. But I'd feel even worse if I thought you were avoiding talking to me about it."

"I really believe you mean that," Nick said.

"I *do!*" Trixie told him.

"That means a lot, Trixie, it really does." Nick's voice suddenly sounded choked. "I'll keep you posted. Good-bye."

Trixie felt tears welling up in her eyes as she hung up the phone. Nick was so grateful for simple friendship, but it was going to take more than friendship to get his family back on track.

The three Beldens walked to the clubhouse in silence. Trixie told her brothers only that Nick had called and that Mr. Roberts had been released. The rest she wanted to hold back until all of the Bob-Whites were together at the clubhouse.

Trixie, Mart, and Brian arrived at the clubhouse at exactly the same time as Jim and Honey.

"Dan and Di can't make it tonight," Jim said. "Dan worked so hard today that he's exhausted. You know how much he and Mr. Maypenny have to do in the spring — clearing paths and shoring up banks that are eroding away and fixing fences."

"Di has to baby-sit," Honey added. "I promised we'd give her a full report tomorrow."

"Let's go inside," Jim said, opening the door and leading the way. "I want to hear about Nick Roberts and his father."

The Bob-Whites trooped into the clubhouse, took cans of soda from the small cooler Mart had carried along, and settled themselves down to discuss the situation.

"I'm not as concerned about Mr. Roberts's legal problems as I was this morning—Pat Murphy will take care of those," Trixie said. "What concerns me is his morale. He just doesn't seem to have the energy to start over."

"It is unfortunate that science has not yet devised a technique that would allow us to reapportion some of our sibling's vim, vigor, and élan," Mart observed, looking at Trixie's shining, earnest-looking face.

"That's true," Jim agreed. "Trixie has enough energy to power a locomotive, if there were only some way to harness it."

"We *all* have energy to spare," Honey said gloomily. "It's just that there's no way to pass it along to Mr. Roberts."

Trixie had been looking increasingly thoughtful ever since Mart's first long-winded observation.

Now, after a moment of silence, she suddenly bounded to her feet and said, "That's it! There is!"

Trixie clenched her hands and jumped up and down. She was afraid that speaking the first word might be like pulling a plug, letting the words pour out in a torrent she couldn't control. Finally, she took a deep breath and began to speak. "Think about it. Money isn't Mr. Roberts's problem — or at least it won't be, if he can stay in business until the real arsonist is caught and the insurance claim is paid. What he needs is the strength to keep going. We Bob-Whites don't have any trouble keeping going, but we *do* have money problems."

"So?" Brian asked, still not seeing the connection.

"S-o-o-o," Trixie said slowly, "there's no reason why we can't work our problems out together. We can sell T-shirts and caps to every softball and baseball team in Sleepyside. Mr. Roberts will stay in business. And the Bob-Whites will *be* in business as far as our summer repairs are concerned, because we'll get a commission on all our sales."

"The Bob-Whites are supposed to devote their time to having fun and helping others," Honey said enthusiastically. "This project sounds like a way to do both. Should we put it to a vote and make it official?"

"Hold on a minute, Sis," Jim said. "We can't just elect ourselves into the job. Mr. Roberts has something to say about it. From what Trixie said, he may very well say 'no.' I think he'd better be consulted before we vote, anyway."

"Oh, woe," Trixie said, suddenly collapsing into a chair. "I *hate* it when real life gets in the way of my perfect dreams. You're right, Jim. Mr. Roberts has the final say over whether or not we go to work for him. He's going to be the hardest sell of all."

"Now, don't go overboard in the other direction, Trixie. Jim wasn't trying to tell you the plan won't work. He just wants you to take things in their proper order. Tomorrow we'll call Nick and tell him our idea. If he goes for it, we'll talk to his father. If *he* goes for it, we'll have a vote, just to make it official. Okay?" Brian asked.

"Nope," Trixie said firmly. "I can't wait until tomorrow to see whether or not I actually can help Nick Roberts. I'm going back home right this minute to call Nick and tell him our plan. You all wait right here."

Before anyone had a chance to object, Trixie was racing out of the clubhouse. Her friends stared at one another in shocked silence as they listened to her feet pounding up the path.

It was Honey who broke the silence by starting

to giggle. As soon as she began to laugh, the three boys did too.

"Ben Franklin said, 'A stitch in time saves nine,'" Jim observed. "At the rate she's going, Trixie will have this deal sewn up in no time."

"And if it's true that only 'she who hesitates is lost,' Trixie will never need a compass," Brian added.

"There is another saying that seems apropos," Mart said. "'Fools rush in where angels fear to tread.'"

When the sandy-haired teenager burst in through the door a few moments later, she was astonished to find her two brothers and her two friends doubled over with laughter. "Well, I'll be," she said. "Here I am, off deciding the future of the Bob-Whites and the Roberts family, and you're in here having a joke-telling contest."

"No, we weren't, Trixie," Honey gasped. "Really, we weren't. We were just — um —" Suddenly realizing that the explanation of what they had been doing wasn't going to make Trixie feel any better, Honey tactfully changed the subject. "Were you able to reach Nick?"

Immediately, Trixie's look of indignation faded and one of excitement took its place. Everyone in the room knew what she was going to say. Still, they waited breathlessly to hear her say it.

"I talked to Nick. He says it's a *great* idea — especially since I explained to him that we really *need* the commission money for the clubhouse. I mean, it was clear to him that we aren't offering charity," Trixie said.

"What about Mr. Roberts?" Jim asked.

"Nick said not to worry about his father. Nick will talk him into it, one way or the other. He says if we'll come over tomorrow, he'll show us the colors and styles that are available and explain the pricing system."

"So it's really settled?" Honey asked.

"All we need is the vote," Trixie answered.

"Call the question," Mart said, using the phrase that meant discussion was ended and a vote must be taken.

"I don't recall that an official motion was made," Jim said with mock-gravity, "let alone seconded. Still, I think that we can dispense with those formalities. Madame Co-Chairperson, would you like to do the honors?"

"I certainly would," Trixie said. "All those in favor of the Bob-Whites becoming Mr. Roberts's summer sales force, so signify by saying 'aye.'"

Five voices chorused, "Aye!"

"Opposed?" Trixie asked.

The question was greeted with resounding silence.

"The motion is carried," Trixie said.

"Yippee!" Honey shouted.

"I had one more idea," Trixie told her friends. "What do you say we have a little contest? The person who sells the most doesn't have to lift a finger when we start painting and puttying the clubhouse."

"Terrific idea!" Jim exclaimed.

"All in favor?" Trixie asked.

Another chorus of "ayes" told her that the Bob-Whites were, indeed, all in favor of the idea.

"Okay," Brian said, "let's get started."

8 * One Clue Lost . . .
One Clue Found

AT ONE O'CLOCK the next afternoon, all seven of the
Bob-Whites were packed into the station wagon
heading for Nick's house. When they pulled into
his driveway, Nick was waiting for them at the side
door. He held the door open while his friends
trooped down the stairs.

Nick had done a good job of setting up a tempo-
rary shop in the basement. The boxes that held the
inventory of caps and shirts were stacked neatly
along the walls. A card table was set up at one end
of the room with pencils, paper, and order forms
waiting and ready.

"I'm going to order a new lettering machine," Nick said. "I'll put it over there, in the one remaining open space."

Trixie noticed that Nick had said "I," not "we." Apparently Mr. Roberts was not yet enthusiastic about the plan. She wondered suddenly if Nick had met them at the door and led them straight to the basement in order to keep them out of his father's way. *It takes a lot of courage to do what Nick is doing*, she thought admiringly.

"Well, let's get started," Nick said. "Here is a set of instructions for each of you, along with some order forms. We have four basic colors — red, blue, green, and yellow. We also have two styles of shirts — T's, with the shorter sleeve, and jerseys, with the longer sleeve. Caps are all one style, and in the same four colors. Prices are noted on your instruction sheets. Now, for the lettering. There are three sizes: one-inch, two-inch, and three-inch. The price is calculated by the letter; the bigger letters cost more, of course. The prices for the various sizes are on the instruction sheets, too. Any questions so far?"

"You've made this so clear that even *I* understand it, Nick," Trixie said, scanning her instruction sheet.

The slender boy smiled appreciatively at Trixie.

"Well, you're pretty understanding, from what I've seen," he said. "For custom work like this, we need ten percent down, at the time you take the orders. That just helps us make sure people are serious about wanting the order. Otherwise, we'd be left with a lot of useless customized merchandise. The balance is C.O.D., which means you get the cash when you deliver the order."

"Cash?" Di asked. "Does that mean you won't take checks?"

"No, no," Nick said hurriedly. "Checks are fine. We don't take credit cards, though. My father doesn't believe in them."

"How's your father doing, by the way?" Brian asked.

Nick's frown contradicted his words: "He's okay."

"Say," Trixie said, "I'd almost forgotten. The story about his release should have been in this morning's paper." Nick's frown deepened so abruptly that she was immediately sorry she'd spoken.

"It was there, all right — two paragraphs on page eight," Nick said.

"That's all!" Honey exclaimed sympathetically.

Nick nodded. "The worst part is that Sergeant Molinson was quoted as saying they released him because they 'didn't have *enough* evidence to press charges.' That made it sound as though there was *some*. That got Dad down pretty badly. I suggested that he and Mother go for a drive this afternoon, just to get away from things for a while."

"That was a good suggestion," Brian said. "And speaking of getting away, that's what we'd better do."

"I'll second that motion," Dan said. "I have some work to do yet this afternoon. I'll be able to start selling first thing tomorrow, though — I have all the information I need."

"We all do," Honey agreed. "You did a perfectly perfect job of organizing everything, Nick."

"There's still one thing you need, though — samples," Nick said. He picked up a box from the floor and opened it to show the Bob-Whites the contents. "There are seven caps and seven T-shirts in here — two each of blue, green, and red, and one yellow. The caps are adjustable, of course. I just guessed at the size of the shirts."

"This is wonderful!" Honey said. "We can wear them whenever we're out selling, so that people will know what the merchandise looks like."

"What if we're selling by phone?" Jim challenged.

"Then we'll wear them to give us confidence," Honey retorted.

"I'm sorry I couldn't imprint them, but I don't

have the equipment I need yet," Nick said.

"We'll take a rain check on that," Brian said as he took the cardboard box from Nick.

"You should make haste in ordering the new equipment, however," Mart said. "You will soon be inundated with orders for individualized apparel."

"You're going to sell lots of merchandise?" Nick guessed.

"You're catching on," Trixie said, laughing. "We'd better get going. Thanks for everything, Nick."

"Thank *you*," he said. He made an "after you" gesture to the Bob-Whites, then followed them up the stairs.

As Jim, who was at the head of the line, opened the side door, the young people heard the sounds of a heated argument coming from the front of the house. The Bob-Whites all hesitated and looked back at Nick, who moved past them and headed for the noise, with the others close behind.

Everyone froze when they saw, on the front walk, Mr. Slettom and Jane Dix-Strauss in a face-to-face confrontation.

"You will leave these people alone, you — you scandal-monger!" Mr. Slettom's face as he yelled was almost as purple as his paisley sports coat.

"That is not your decision to make," Jane Dix-Strauss retorted. "If Nicholas Roberts doesn't want to talk to me, let him tell me so himself."

"Will you take my word for it?" Nick asked, walking slowly toward the two. "I'm Nicholas Roberts's son, and I know he doesn't want to talk to you."

"That's right, Nick," Mr. Slettom said. "Don't let this woman do any more harm to your father."

"*I* haven't harmed your father," Jane Dix-Strauss retorted. "Circumstances have. I want to hear his side of the story. I want to make sure it gets printed."

"Sure," Nick said, his face suddenly hard. "You can print it on page eight, the way you did the story of his release. Maybe you can even give him three paragraphs, instead of two."

"The release story was different — it wasn't *news*. An interview with a suspect would be," Jane Dix-Strauss said heatedly.

"So you admit you suspect my father," Nick accused.

"No!" Jane Dix-Strauss said. "But *you* have to admit that your father *is* a suspect."

"Thanks to you!" Mr. Slettom told her.

"Please!" Nick said loudly. "My father isn't here right now, anyway. Mr. Slettom, I'm sure he'd be happy to talk to you later, if you'd like to call him. Miss Dix-Strauss, I really don't think that Dad will let you interview him."

"All right," the reporter said. "I'll just have to get the information some other way." She turned and went back down the walk.

Mr. Slettom watched her go, a look of satisfaction on his face. "Good work, Nick," he said. "I wish I'd been able to chase her off before she disturbed you, though. I'm glad your father wasn't home."

"Well, I'm sorry *you* missed him," Nick said.

"No problem, no problem," Mr. Slettom said with a wave of his hand. "I just wanted to stop by and see how he was doing. I can do that another day. So long."

Trixie was still staring at Jane Dix-Strauss, who was unlocking the door of a red compact car. *That woman!* she thought angrily, jamming her clenched fists into the pockets of her jacket. *Who does she think she is, anyway?* Trixie's hand touched a small, hard object. *The button!* she thought. *Maybe I can use it to ruffle those smooth feathers of hers.* She hurried down the walk and reached the little car just as Jane Dix-Strauss was starting the engine with one hand and rolling down the window with the other.

"Excuse me," Trixie said. "I think I have something of yours." She held the button out on her outstretched palm.

Jane Dix-Strauss took it. She looked down at it for a moment, then looked up at Trixie, obviously startled. "Where did you find this?"

"In the alley behind Mr. Roberts's store. It was under an old brick. Don't you remember losing it there?" Trixie asked pointedly.

"No, I don't." The woman hesitated for a moment. She seemed to be on the verge of saying something. Then, abruptly, her face resumed its cool and composed look. "Thank you very much," she said. She dropped the button into the pocket of her blazer and, without giving Trixie another look, put the car into gear and drove away.

Trixie stood and watched the little red car. Her mouth had dropped open, and her cheeks were flaming red. *She took it! My only clue, and she grabbed it right out of my hand and drove off with it!* Then Trixie's jaw tightened as her anger suddenly turned inward. *Well, what was I expecting her to do? I held the button out to her and told her I knew it was hers. I all but invited her to take it! Some detective I am!*

"What was that all about, Trix?"

Trixie turned at the sound of Jim's voice and saw

that all the Bob-Whites were walking toward her. "Oh, I-I just wanted to ask her something."

She hoped the matter would drop there, but Jim asked, "What?"

"Oh — uh — just one of the figures in one of her stories," Trixie said hastily. "You remember, Brian and Mart, how she wrote that there's a billion dollars worth of arson every year? I've been wondering if that really was *billion* — with a *b*."

"And was it?" Jim asked.

"Jane Dix-Strauss would never write anything that wasn't true." She said it in a tone of exaggerated innocence. *I hope no one notices I didn't really answer Jim's question*, she thought.

"Let's go, you guys," Dan Mangan said impatiently. "I have work to do."

Saved! Trixie thought, turning quickly away from her curious brothers and walking toward the car.

Honey hurriedly fell in step with her. "You asked her about the button, didn't you?" she whispered.

Trixie nodded. "Boy, was she ever surprised!" she whispered back.

"Did she admit losing it in the alley?" Honey asked.

"Not exactly," Trixie said. Then, having to be

honest with her best friend, she added, "Not at all. She took the button, too. Now there's no evidence against her."

"We'll find some," Honey said confidently, linking her arm through Trixie's. "If Jane Dix-Strauss is guilty of something, we'll prove it."

"What's all the whispering about?" Jim asked, quickening his pace to overtake them and unlock the car door.

"We're just figuring out how to sell the most T-shirts *and* do the least painting," Trixie said. *I'm not really lying*, she thought, *just teasing*.

"Nick certainly told us everything we need to know," Honey said.

"What Nick told us represents only an introduction to the art of solicitation," Mart said as he climbed into the car. "I intend to take myself to the library tomorrow to get some books on the subject, the better to represent both Mr. Roberts and the Bob-Whites. And the better to avoid the agony of work later this summer."

"Can I come along?" Trixie asked impulsively.

"What?" Mart asked. "You want to accompany me to a site of mental edification?"

"Don't act as if I'd never been to the library before, Mart Belden," Trixie told him. "If I hadn't been, Honey and I would never have figured out how to find Regan when he ran away to Saratoga that time. But if you don't want to be seen with me, I'll just go by myself."

"I would by no means forfeit the opportunity to be seen in your company on this rare — albeit, as you point out, not unique — occasion," Mart said.

The subject was changed, and Trixie thought it had been forgotten. That night, however, Brian came into her room. "It really isn't like you to want to read up on a subject before you plunge into it, Trix," he said. There was no teasing in his tone, just gentle concern. "How come you're not in your 'let's get started' mode any more?"

"Well, there is a lot to learn, as Mart pointed out," Trixie said. As her oldest brother continued to gaze levelly at her, she confessed, "Oh, Brian, all of a sudden I got cold feet. Seeing Jane Dix-Strauss reminded me that, thanks to her, Mr. Roberts is still suspect number one. I started wondering how people will treat his summer sales force. I guess I'm hoping that doing some reading on the subject of selling will give me some pointers to build up my confidence."

"That sounds like an excellent reason for going to the library," Brian said quietly. "I wish you the best of luck."

Since Mart's junior driver's license permitted

him to drive only when accompanied by an adult, Mart and Trixie had to use their bicycles as their means of transportation into Sleepyside. Neither of the young people minded that, since it was a sunny June day, with just enough breeze to cool them off without slowing them down.

Inside the library Trixie followed Mart as he took a card tray out of the cabinet and walked over to the table with it.

"Here is the correct topical notation," Mart said. "'Sales.' There are two appropriate subcategories, as well: 'Successful Selling' and 'Careers in Sales.'"

"You mean all those books are on selling?" Trixie asked. "Why, that row of cards must be six inches long!"

"At least," Mart agreed. "Obviously you have never thought about the crucial role that selling plays in our society. Why, the chair you are sitting on, the table on which your elbows rest, the card file, and the cards themselves, not to mention the books, are in this library solely because someone sold them to someone else."

"Gleeps, you're right," Trixie said. "I never thought about that before. I just thought that whenever someone needed something, they went out and bought it, the way I do."

"Such naiveté," Mart said. "You 'just go out and buy it,' do you? Tell me, to whom do you inquire about prices or alternate styles or colors?"

Trixie sighed, signaling her defeat. "A salesperson," she admitted.

"Precisely. And does that person never suggest that you buy the more expensive item, or buy two while they're on sale, or buy a pair of stockings to accompany the purchase of a new pair of shoes?"

Trixie nodded without speaking, knowing that Mart knew what her answer would be.

"*That* is salesmanship. A worthy career and, at its best, an art. That is what we are here to learn. Now," he said, rising from the table with his list of books in hand, "while I check on the availability of these books, why don't you look at the periodicals? Some shorter but more current information might be available there."

Obediently, Trixie went to the shelf where the volumes of *The Readers' Guide to Periodical Literature* were kept. Mart had said he wanted current information from the magazines, so she ignored the fat, hard-bound volumes from earlier years and looked in the paper-bound volumes that represented recent months. She looked under *Sales*, *Selling*, and, directed by those two categories, under *Marketing* as well. Altogether there were five or six promising-sounding articles. Dutifully, she wrote the name of the magazine, its date, the volume, and the page of the article on the preprinted request slips. She brought the slips to the librarian and was told she'd have to wait a few minutes for the magazines.

Trixie stood impatiently in front of the desk. Feeling that it was rude to be so obviously impatient, she wandered back to the reference table and sat down. She dragged out one of the green volumes of the *Readers' Guide* and leafed through it idly. *Doing research isn't really that hard,* she thought. *Not if the topic is interesting. I guess I can see how Jane Dix-Strauss came up with information on arson so quickly.* As she thought that, she turned to the front of the volume and looked up *Arson.* A month before she might have been surprised at the number of articles under the heading. Now she knew only too well how common a crime it was. Somehow, though, one article caught her eye.

"'Anatomy of Arson, by Jane Dix-Strauss,'" Trixie read aloud. "Well, I'll be!" The magazine in which the article had been published was a well-known one. There was no doubt that the library would have it. Trixie scribbled out another request slip and hurried up to the librarian with it.

When the magazine came, Trixie hurried off with it, barely remembering in time to come back and get the stack of magazines with salesmanship articles that she'd originally requested. She found a secluded table and turned to the article the new *Sun* reporter had written two years before.

It didn't take Trixie long to feel as though she had read the article before. All of the facts and figures were included in Jane Dix-Strauss's coverage of the Memorial Day fire.

Even more exciting to Trixie, the article contained many quotes from interviews Jane Dix-Strauss had conducted with arsonists. Some were in jail, serving time for the fires they had set. Remarkably, other arsonists were confidential sources who admitted they had set fires but had never been caught!

Trixie gathered up her stack of magazines again and went off to find Mart. He had a huge stack of books on selling on a table in front of him, and he was hurriedly going through them, trying to winnow their number into something he could manage on a bicycle.

"Mart, look at this!" Trixie said, shoving the magazine in front of his nose.

Mart read in silence for a moment. "Hmm," he

said, finally. "Very interesting. You have, as usual, been involved in sleuthing. I'd say you've done an excellent job of unraveling the mystery of how Jane Dix-Strauss was able to publish so many facts on arson so quickly."

"You're missing the whole point, Mart," Trixie hissed. "I don't think this article solves any mysteries. I think it *creates* some. Look — Jane Dix-Strauss wrote this article that was published in a big national magazine two years ago. Now she comes to work at the dinky little *Sleepyside Sun*. Why the comedown? Then, even though there's never been a case of arson in town, weeks after she comes to work here, there is one! Do you think that's just coincidence?"

"I certainly do," Mart said. "What did you find on the more salubrious subject of selling?"

Trixie slapped the other magazines down on the table in front of Mart. "Do you have any change?" she asked. "I want to make a copy of this article."

Distractedly, his mind already on the magazine articles on selling, Mart dug a handful of change out of his pocket and handed it to his sister. When she returned with the photocopied article, he had returned most of the books and all of the magazines. What remained he was stuffing into his backpack. "I have selected sufficient data with which to make my start. Shall we proceed homeward?" he said.

"Absolutely," Trixie agreed, eager to show her article to the one person in the world who might possibly feel the same way about it.

9 * Selling and Sleuthing

"WELL, HONEY?" Trixie asked after her friend had read the article. "Does it seem like a coincidence to you?"

"N-no," Honey said. "But, Trixie, it has to be. Otherwise — I mean, you can't think Jane Dix-Strauss set those fires herself, just to give herself something to write about. Can you?"

"Wel-l-l." Now it was Trixie's turn to hesitate. Her friend's honest question made Trixie see how farfetched her suspicions sounded.

"Even if, somehow, it were true, what can we do?" Honey asked.

Trixie's answer was not, strictly speaking, to Honey's question. It was a response to all of the frustrating, unprovable suspicions she'd been having all day. "All we can do is sell T-shirts," she said grimly.

To Trixie's surprise, selling T-shirts soon became an enthralling part of the summer. Brian made the first sale, and it was a good one. The camp where he and Mart had worked as summer counselors ordered two hundred shirts, all printed with the camp name and logo.

"So," Brian said, writing up the order on the order pads Nick had given them, "although writing up a sale this big is a strain on the wrist, it's comforting to know I won't be overworking it with a paintbrush later this summer."

Trixie was just opening her mouth to retort — although she hadn't yet decided what she'd say — when the phone rang. *Saved by the bell*, she thought as she went to answer it.

"Hi, it's me," Jim said. He was so jubilant that Trixie had no doubts about what he was going to say. "I got an order! The Big Wheels ordered thirty shirts *with* matching hats. Not bad, huh?"

"Not bad," Trixie agreed reluctantly. "But who are the Big Wheels?"

"They're the softball team my father sponsors,"

Jim said. "Matthew Wheeler's Big Wheels — get the joke?"

"I get the joke," Trixie said wearily.

"And I got the order," Jim told her again. "Mustn't rest on my laurels, though. One order won't be enough to get me out of painting this summer."

Trixie went back into the living room to tell her brothers about Jim's good news. "But," she said, "I don't think it's fair. Jim's order and yours, Brian, were from personal friends. That shouldn't count."

"Why in the world not?" Brian asked.

"Well, because — then it's more charity than real salesmanship that makes people place the order," Trixie said.

"You think the people at camp bought two hundred T-shirts they didn't need just because I used to work there as a junior counselor? Come on, Trix!" Brian chided her.

"Personal rapport with the prospect is one of the cardinal rules of the profession," Mart said. "In fact, it's the primary rule given in many of the books I read. They advise that the novice seller sit down and make a list of everyone he or she knows. That includes people in the same clubs, people from the same neighborhood, even — or maybe especially — people from whom you buy things. Insurance salespeople will call on their car dealers, and car dealers will call on the people who sold them their homes, and so forth."

"Well, I don't have a car or a house or any insurance, so how does your selling theory help me? I don't know *anybody*," Trixie said.

"Oh, come on," Brian retorted. "Supersleuth Trixie? You know more people than the rest of us put together. I think you're just scared of selling."

"Scared? Me?" Trixie asked indignantly. Then her shoulders fell forward and she said, "You're right. I am a little scared. I keep thinking that people will hang up on me or laugh at me."

"Well, they won't," Brian said. "You know what I think your problem is? You're not keeping your eye on the ball."

"Huh?" Trixie wrinkled her nose and squinted at her oldest brother. She had accepted that advice from him in softball and golf. But what did it have to do with selling?

"In this case," Brian explained, "the ball is the product — Nick's T-shirts and caps. Do you think they're good products?"

"Of course!" Trixie said.

"Do you think they're reasonably priced?" Brian asked.

"Yes, certainly," Trixie said.

"Do you believe Nick will deliver the product on time?" Brian continued.

"Absolutely!" Trixie said.

"Well, if you call and offer people a well-made, reasonably priced item that they can get when they need it, why would those people hang up on you?" Brian concluded. "That's what I mean by taking your eye off the ball. You'll only get scared if you're thinking too much about yourself and not enough about what you're trying to sell."

"I get it, Brian. Thanks!" Trixie turned and marched back to the phone, picked up the receiver before she could stop to think, and dialed a familiar number.

Within a few minutes, she was back, a beaming smile on her face. "Well, that's it — I got my first order," she said.

"Great, Trixie," Brian said sincerely. "Who is it from?"

"Bruce Becker at Dad's bank," Trixie said. "He's captain of their softball team. I noticed last year that their uniforms were a little ragged-looking. When I called to ask if he wanted to order new T-shirts, he was positively grateful! Selling is easy!"

Trixie looked at her brothers for further approval, but they looked more irritated than proud.

"Our sister the shamus has unraveled the mysteries of salesmanship," Mart said. "No prospect will be safe from her clutches hereafter."

"Me and my big mouth," Brian said. "I just wish I'd waited to explain the secrets of selling until *after* I'd called Bruce Becker. He was on my list."

"Oh, Brian, I'm sorry," Trixie said. "I should have asked you before I called the bank. Would you like to write up the order?"

"No, Trixie. You made the sale; you write up the order. All's fair in sales and war," Brian reassured her. "Don't tell anyone whom you're going to call. We should all tell one another whom we *have* called, though — we don't want to drive anyone to distraction with calls about T-shirts."

"Whatever you say," Trixie told him cheerfully as she sat down at the table to write up the order.

The Bob-Whites wrote up many orders in the following days. Using Mart's selling tip, they all were able to think of lots of people who were in need of their product.

"Part of it is that we timed it just about right," Trixie told Nick one night when she was phoning in the day's orders. "All the sports teams are just starting up, and they've just noticed how crummy their uniforms look. I don't think that's all of it, though. I think lots of people are ordering from

us because they want to help your father. Just
about all the people I talk to ask how he is and
say they're glad the fire didn't knock him out of
business."

"People are being really good to us," Nick
agreed. "We're getting direct calls for products,
too. Even Mr. Slettom ordered shirts for the softball team his appliance store sponsors."

"Isn't that great?" Trixie asked. Without waiting
for an answer, she added, "How *is* your father doing, Nick?"

"He's better, I think," Nick said. "The caring
and concern is the best medicine he could have.
Besides, all these orders are spurring his work
ethic. He's too worried about letting his customers
down to worry about his own problems."

"That's just what we'd hoped, isn't it?" Trixie
said. "Well, I'd better not tie up the phone lines
any longer. We've probably missed orders for hundreds of shirts already!" Trixie could hear Nick
chuckling as she hung up the phone.

She turned and started away, then turned back
as the phone began to ring. She picked it up and
said, "Hello?"

"Hello?" a voice on the other end of the line
responded. "Are you the people who are selling
T-shirts?"

"Yes, we are," Trixie said promptly.

"Well, I'd like to order thirty shirts that say 'Carlson Classic Invitational Horseshoe Tournament' on the back. Can I have them by the Fourth of July?"

"Gleeps!" Trixie said. "Do you know how much that's going to cost?"

"Why, n-no," said the voice. "That's why I called *you*."

Trixie hesitated. A fine salesperson she had turned out to be! Now, any price was going to sound expensive to the caller, because she had assured him it would be! She cleared her throat nervously and did some rapid calculations. The resulting amount did seem astronomical, and when she told the caller what it was, he agreed.

"Doggone it," he said. "I really did want something to make this year's tournament special. But I can't afford to pay that much. It's just a family event."

Hearing the genuine concern in her caller's voice, Trixie forgot her nervousness. "There must be something we can do," she said. "How about caps? They're less expensive."

"I wanted something that could be imprinted, though," the caller said.

"The caps can be imprinted," Trixie told him.

"Not with 'Carlson Classic Invitational Horse-shoe Tournament,'" the caller pointed out.

"Well, no," Trixie admitted. "But we could just use an abbreviation, like 'CC,' and the year. The people at the tournament will know what it means, and when they wear the cap afterward, people will ask and they can explain."

"That sounds good," the caller said enthusiastically. "Write it up."

"Right you are!" Trixie said joyfully.

Trixie told Honey the story that evening as they biked into Sleepyside. "It's just like Brian said the first day," she concluded. "If I keep my mind on the customers' problems and how my product can help solve them, I'm not nervous at all!"

"Still, though, it was really clever of you to suggest the caps after the T-shirts were too expensive," Honey said.

"You must be the clever one," Trixie said. "You're ahead in the contest so far!"

"That's been mostly luck," Honey said modestly. "I started out calling everyone from school that I could think of who was on a summer sports team. But what really put me ahead was the woman ordering seventy-five T-shirts for her family reunion. They all are to say, 'Proud to be a Barti-

kowski,' and all that lettering is enough to put anyone ahead!"

"Gosh," Trixie said, "I hope nobody at the reunion is a size small — there won't be room for all
that on a T-shirt. They'll have to put the extra letters on a hankie that they can carry along!"

That thought made the two girls start laughing
so hard that they had to pull their bikes over to the
side of the road. When they were finally on their
way again, Trixie said, "I think it's going to seem
real to me tonight for the first time. When we go to
Nick's, I'll really *see* my very first order. Then I'll
get to make my very first delivery."

"The way it's worked out is perfectly perfect,"
Honey added. "I think it was wonderful of Bruce
Becker to make the new shirts a surprise and ask
us to deliver them to the softball diamond just before the game."

Trixie and Honey had to hurry to get to Nick's
house, pick up the shirts, and get to the softball diamond in time, but they made it. They handed the
two big bags over to Bruce Becker, who called his
team together and, with a flourish, pulled out one
of the shirts and held it up.

A cheer went up from the team, and everyone
grabbed for the shirts at once. There was a lot of
trading back and forth until everyone found the

right size. Then the old shirts were peeled off, and the new shirts were pulled on.

Within a few minutes, the whole team was arrayed in vivid blue.

"Well, Trixie, if we play as well as we look, we can't lose," Bruce Becker told her.

Trixie and Honey stayed to watch the game. Sure enough, the Sleepyside Bankers beat the opposing team easily. Afterward, the Bankers sent up a shout of "T-shirts, T-shirts, T-shirts!" that had Trixie and Honey clutching their sides with laughter once again.

"Well, that's that," Trixie said as they pedaled home. "My first sale, my first delivery, and my first satisfied customers."

"If they'd all be that good, we'd never want to stop selling," Honey said.

The girls rode slowly back through town toward Glen Road. The evening was pleasantly warm and there was almost no breeze at all.

Suddenly Trixie sat up straight on her bike. "Honey, I just thought of something. You haven't seen Mr. Roberts's store since the fire. Let's ride past it now on our way home."

"Do you really think that's a good idea, Trixie?" Honey asked. "It's starting to get dark, and that store isn't in a very good part of town."

"It isn't *that* dark," Trixie said. "It won't take a minute."

"Wel-l-l," Honey drawled. She was curious, and she was also unable to resist her best friend's wishes for very long. "All right," she said finally.

A few minutes later, the two girls stood looking at the burned-out building. "It looks so little to have held such a big explosion," Honey said.

"It caused such big problems, too," Trixie added. She shook her head. "When I was here before, Brian said the fire takes some getting used to. But I just can't. It keeps seeming more *un*real and more ridiculous."

"Ridiculous?" Honey echoed. "That's a funny word to use."

"I don't mean that the fire itself was ridiculous," Trixie said. "I just mean the setting of it was. This building is too small to be worth much in insurance. It's in too shabby a neighborhood to be worth remodeling. It's too ordinary to inspire revenge in anybody. Why bother to burn it down?"

"I don't know," Honey admitted. Seeing Trixie get off her bike and push the kickstand down with her foot, she added, "What are you doing?"

"I'm just going to take another look around," Trixie said. "You said if there was any more evidence against Jane Dix-Strauss, we'd find it. How can we find it if we don't look?"

"But *you* said we wouldn't stay long," Honey reminded her friend. "It's getting darker by the minute. Nick said they had mice even when there were people in the building. Now that it's abandoned, there are probably rats — maybe even bats," Honey added with a shudder. "Come on, Trixie. We can come back tomorrow when it's light out."

"That's silly, Honey," Trixie said. "It's a long bike ride to get here. Besides, our days are too busy already with the sales and the regular chores. We'd never find time to get back. I just want to walk around the building one more time. Do you want to come along or wait here?"

Honey frowned. "I don't want to do either," she said. "I want to go home."

"We *will*," Trixie said. "We'll be on our way in ten minutes — no more, I promise. Do you want to come along?"

"No," Honey said. She sounded both frightened and angry at the stubbornness of her friend.

Trixie heard the anger, but she couldn't let it stop her. Something irresistible was drawing her toward the deserted, boarded-up building. "I'll be right back," she said as reassuringly as she could.

Cautiously, Trixie made her way to the alley in the back of the building. She started around the corner, then froze, her blood turning cold, when she saw two figures standing in the alley.

Trixie pulled herself back into the shadow of the building and stared at the two people. They were standing face-to-face, obviously talking, although Trixie could not hear what they were saying. The person on the left was a man — a big one, both tall and broad. He was wearing a short jacket, with the collar turned up around his face.

The person on the right was a woman. Trixie gasped when she recognized who it was. She strained her eyes through the deepening gloom to be sure.

There could be no doubt. The woman standing here behind Mr. Roberts's store was Jane Dix-Strauss!

10 * Was It a Payoff?

TRIXIE SQUEEZED HER EYES SHUT for a second, then opened them and looked again. Now she was sure. Even in the dim light, the reporter's slim figure and dark, curly hair were easy to recognize.

Before Trixie had time to wonder what to do, Jane Dix-Strauss's voice was suddenly raised, carrying across the distance to where Trixie was hiding. "All right," she said. "That's it, then. If I need anything else, I'll call." As she spoke, the reporter reached into the pocket of her blazer and pulled out something. *A folded piece of paper,* Trixie thought, *or maybe — yes, that's it — an envelope.*

The man muttered something. Because his back was turned, Trixie could pick up only the sound of his voice, not the words. He took the envelope and tucked it into an inside pocket of his coat.

Trixie watched what was happening as if it were a scene on stage. Gradually, she began to realize that this was not play-acting. It was real life, which meant that she was eavesdropping. She should clear her throat or make some noise to let the two people in the alley know she was there. That somehow seemed the fairest thing to do. But as Trixie thought about her previous encounters with Jane Dix-Strauss, the idea of the brusque young woman appreciating the fairness seemed ridiculous. More likely, she'd yell at Trixie for peeping. Maybe she'd demand to know how long Trixie had been standing there and what she'd heard.

Or maybe she'd offer to pay me off, too, Trixie thought. The thought startled her. Some part of her mind had put the white envelope together with the idea of a payoff. *Is that what it is?* she asked herself. *Is Jane Dix-Strauss paying that man off for something? For what?*

The thought distracted Trixie, momentarily, from her worries about whether or not to let her presence be known. And suddenly the problem was taken out of her hands.

"Trixie!" Honey's voice floated back, not loudly but quite clearly, from the sidewalk in front of the building. "Trixie, it's getting dark! Let's go!"

Trixie froze, her ears listening to Honey's call, her eyes glued to Jane Dix-Strauss and the mysterious man.

"What's that?" the woman asked.

Trixie waited just long enough to see the two begin to turn in her direction. That was it — she couldn't hope to find out anything more by waiting around. In a moment, she'd be found out herself. She started walking back to the sidewalk as quickly and quietly as she could.

"We've got to get out of here," she told Honey. She grabbed her bike and kicked at the kickstand clumsily, needing three tries to get it out of the way of the pedal.

"What happened?" Honey asked.

"I can't explain now," Trixie said as she threw her leg over the seat of the bike and pushed down on the pedal. "Just hurry — let's get out of here."

Honey didn't ask any more questions. In a split second, she was on her bike. The two girls pedaled furiously, their bodies bent low over the handlebars to increase their speed.

Trixie led her friend to Main Street and headed out on Glen Road. By now it was almost dark. For the sake of safety, Honey hung back so that both girls could stay well off the road. It was the right thing to do, Trixie knew — but she wished that Honey would ignore safety, just this once. She was bursting to tell her best friend what had happened behind Mr. Roberts's store.

The girls rode directly to Crabapple Farm. They ran up the stairs hoping that they wouldn't be way-laid by Mart, Brian, or Bobby. Soon, however, they were safely behind Trixie's closed door.

Honey plopped herself down on the bed and gave an excited bounce. "Now, tell me this very minute, Trixie Belden. What happened back in that alley?"

"You aren't going to believe it, Honey," Trixie said, flopping down on her stomach beside her friend. She closed her eyes and pictured the scene again. "I came around the corner, and I froze because I saw two people standing there. One of them was this enormous man — six feet four, at least, and *big*. The other person was smaller. And female. And someone I'd seen before. Someone you've seen, too." Trixie opened one eye and peered at her friend. Now that the danger was past, she was enjoying the telling of it.

"Who?" Honey squealed impatiently.

"Sleepyside's star reporter, that's who," Trixie said smugly.

"Jane Dix-Strauss?" Honey asked.

"None other," Trixie said.

"What were they doing back there?" Honey asked.

"Well, when I first saw them, I think they were talking, but I couldn't hear what they were saying. But *then*" — Trixie sat up on the bed, the better to add gestures to the story — "Jane Dix-Strauss said, 'That's it, then. If I need anything else, I'll call.' And she reached into her blazer pocket, and she took out an envelope, and she handed it to the man, and he put it into his pocket!"

As Trixie finished speaking, silence fell over the room.

"And then?" Honey asked finally.

Trixie sat back in amazement. "Oh, Honey, don't you see? It was a payoff!"

"A payoff." Honey repeated the words without conviction.

"It has to be," Trixie continued. "Jane Dix-Strauss is in the alley behind the burned-out building with this mysterious man. She hands him an envelope. It can't be something regular, like a letter, because she could just mail it. It has to be something she'd want kept secret — like a payoff for something. And what would she be paying somebody off for behind Roberts's store?"

"Some photographs he took for her?" Honey asked helpfully.

"Photographs!" Trixie said. "In the dark? Besides, Jane Dix-Strauss takes her own pictures. Don't you remember how she sneaked up on us with her camera at the Memorial Day parade?"

"Well, *what* then?" Honey's usually limitless patience was wearing thin.

"*I* think she was paying off the arsonist," Trixie said, dropping her voice to a whisper.

"What!" All Honey could do was to squeak the word.

"Well, think about it," Trixie said reasonably. "Jane Dix-Strauss is already an expert on arson. As soon as she moves here, Sleepyside has a case of arson. The result is that this new reporter gets some articles with her by-line on the front page. Overnight she's a star."

"So you think she paid an arsonist to set the fire?" Honey asked, not sounding at all convinced.

"We know she knows arsonists," Trixie said. "She quoted lots of them in that article."

"She quoted lots of fire marshals and police detectives, too," Honey reminded her. "Maybe that's who she was talking to."

"Why meet a fire marshal at night?" Trixie countered. "Why stand and talk to him in the alley? Besides, fire marshals and detectives are public employees. They can't take payoffs from a reporter."

"But you don't know that this *was* a payoff, Trixie — not really," Honey said defensively. Always loyal, Honey was pained by her inability to side with Trixie's version of what had happened.

"Well, if it wasn't a payoff, what was it?" Trixie asked.

"I don't know," Honey said. She thought for a moment. "Maybe it was a list of questions about the fire that she wanted the fire marshal to answer."

"Then why would she say, 'I'll call you if I need you' when she gave him the envelope? That made it sound like they were finished with their business, not like they were right in the middle of it."

"But if the man *was* the arsonist," Honey said, "their business together was over weeks ago — as soon as the fire started, in fact. Why wait this long to pay him off?"

It was Trixie's turn to sit in silence thinking about the question. "Maybe she wasn't going to pay him at all," she said finally. "The arsonist did bungle the job, you know. Maybe"—Trixie pulled herself up to her knees on the bed as she warmed to her own theory—"maybe the fire was supposed to look accidental, and then Jane Dix-Strauss could prove it was arson, so she could look like a hero. So when the arsonist bungled it, she told him she wasn't going to pay. But he threatened her, and said he'd beat her up or even *kill* her if she didn't pay up."

"That's possible, I suppose," Honey conceded. "But then what about that button you found in the alley? If she hired someone else to set the fire, then when did she lose that button? Or doesn't the button mean anything any more?"

"I don't know," Trixie said. She sagged back against the headboard of her bed. Her efforts to convince Honey had left her feeling tired.

"We could tell the story to someone else," Honey volunteered. "Just because I'm not convinced doesn't mean no one else will be."

"Oh, come on, Honey. You're always the first person in the world to believe me. Sometimes you're the *only* one. If you don't agree with my version of things, do you think Brian would? Or Jim? Or *Mart?*" As she said his name, she wrinkled her nose.

In spite of the seriousness of the situation, Honey started to giggle. "If you came up with a theory that the sky was blue, Mart would demand more proof," she admitted.

Trixie laughed, too, shaking her head at the same time. "Brian and Jim aren't much better, though. Adults are lots *worse.* All they ever think about is whether what I'm telling them is dangerous — not whether it's true."

"Well, sometimes we *do* give them reason for worrying," Honey admitted. After another pause, she asked, "What do we do now, Trixie?"

Trixie shrugged. "Nothing, I guess. There's nobody to tell about what I saw, and nothing to do about it. I guess we'll just keep it in mind, and wait."

"Wait for what?" Honey asked.

Again, Trixie shrugged. Then, suddenly, she jumped to her feet. "Oh, Honey, I *do* know!"

"What?" Honey demanded.

"Let's just suppose I'm right — that Jane Dix-Strauss hired an arsonist to set that fire so she'd have big news to write about. The fire won't be big news forever. What happens when everyone forgets about it?"

"You don't think she'd have another fire set, do you?" Honey asked in dismay.

"Another fire — or something," Trixie said.

"Oh, Trixie, you can't really think that."

"I probably couldn't," Trixie told her, "if I hadn't heard what she said to that man: 'I'll call you if I need anything else.'"

When Honey left for home a few minutes later, the two girls were no closer to deciding on a plan of action. *Unless you count deciding to do nothing as a plan of action,* Trixie thought. She stayed in her room with the door closed. She didn't trust herself *not* to tell her brothers about the scene behind Mr. Roberts's store, but she didn't feel like facing their disbelief, which would be so much stronger than Honey's.

For once, she was glad when bedtime came. She was sure she'd sleep well after her frantic bike ride. Instead, sleep came fitfully. She kept half waking from dreams she couldn't remember. Toward morning, her dream took her back to the night of the Memorial Day fire. Once again she was in the throng of people on Main Street. Once again she could hear the sirens and see the fire truck, so close to the orange glow rising in the sky, but not close enough, and not able to get any closer. In her dream, she turned her back on the fire truck and put her hands over her ears. It didn't help — the sirens were still just as loud.

Trixie woke with a start and felt a flood of relief when she saw her own room, with sunlight coming in through the windows. *It was just a dream,* she reassured herself.

Then, suddenly, she knew it hadn't been — not altogether. Now she was wide awake, but she could still hear the sirens!

11 * "We're Going to the Police!"

TRIXIE THREW BACK THE SHEET, jumped out of bed, and got into jeans and a T-shirt. She splashed some water on her face and ran a comb through her hair, then ran down the stairs.

All the while, the sirens kept going. She wasn't surprised, therefore, to see her parents and her two older brothers listening to the radio when she got downstairs.

"What is it?" she demanded. "What's —"

"Sh!" Brian said, making a "keep it quiet" gesture with one hand.

". . . is the second large fire in Sleepyside in less than a month," the radio announcer was saying.

"Oh, no!" Trixie said, sinking into a chair and covering her eyes with her hands. Through her self-imposed darkness, the radio announcer's voice sounded even more ominous.

"The fire is thought to have started at around seven-thirty A.M., when the store was unoccupied, so there were no injuries. A passing patrol officer spotted the smoke and called the fire department. The fire fighters arrived quickly at the scene, but the fire had spread quickly, causing massive damage to the store."

"What store?" Trixie asked, raising her head and looking around for an answer.

Another "pipe down" signal from Brian was the only response in the room, but the radio announcer soon filled in the missing information. ". . . a complete loss, according to Mr. James D. Slettom, owner of the appliance store," the voice said calmly.

Trixie shuddered. "Mr. Slettom?" she echoed. "Is that *the* Mr. Slettom? The one who owned Mr. Roberts's store, too?"

Again the radio announcer provided the answer: ". . . marking the second time in a month that property owned by Mr. Slettom has been the scene of a major fire. Stay tuned to WSTH for further developments."

As a commercial began, Mart got up and turned off the radio. Mrs. Belden went into the kitchen to make breakfast. Mr. Belden went upstairs to shave and finish getting ready for work — a task he'd interrupted at the sound of the sirens. Brian went to the front door and brought in the morning paper.

"At least this fire happened too late for Jane Dix-Strauss to get a scoop on it for the *Sun*," he said. "That should make you happy, Trix."

For the first time that morning, Trixie remembered the scene she'd witnessed the night before: Jane Dix-Strauss and the mysterious man behind Mr. Roberts's store. She remembered, too, one of the questions Honey had asked: "If the man was the arsonist, why would Jane Dix-Strauss wait so long before she paid him?"

It had been a question Trixie didn't have an answer for at the time. But this morning, a simple explanation came to her mind. *What if it wasn't that fire she was paying him for?*

The idea of it made Trixie gasp. As her brothers turned to look at her, she covered it with a hasty yawn. "Those sirens woke me out of a sound sleep," she said.

"I wish I were privileged to indulge in such prolonged slumbers," Mart said pompously. "I, of course, have more pressing pursuits to attend to. I expect to equalize the situation by relaxing when the efforts at the clubhouse commence."

"Oh, fiddledeedee." Trixie knew it wasn't a very impressive counterargument, but it was too early, and she had too much on her mind, to do better. "Anyway, you guys knocked off early yesterday, while Honey and I did some of the most effective legwork we could have done." She told her brothers about delivering the T-shirts to the Sleepyside Bankers. "They loved their shirts, so by today we should have customers running after *us*," she said smugly.

"Hmm," Brian said as he walked to the table which Mrs. Belden had set for breakfast. "Not bad technique, at that. I'll have to remember it. I was wondering where you and Honey were last night. I'm glad you were working on the project at hand and not looking for a mystery to jump into headfirst."

For a moment, Trixie concentrated very hard on pouring milk on her cereal. If only Brian knew that that's *exactly* what they had been doing! She wondered if she should tell him — or someone — as she'd said she would if another arson took place. But something made her hesitate. *I said it had to be another arson before I'd speak up*, she reasoned silently. *I don't know yet that this was arson, which is exactly what Brian and Mart would tell me if I tried to tell them about it. So I won't— until I know something more.*

By noon, Trixie knew more than she wanted to know. The fire had quickly been labeled arson by the investigators. As they had reconstructed the crime, someone had broken into the store by the back door, scattered the store's records around the office, and set them on fire.

But the news on the radio was even worse. "Mr. Nicholas Roberts, who was questioned about the earlier fire and released, was seen in the vicinity of the Slettom Appliance Store early this morning," the radio announcer said. "Police are questioning Roberts again. Sources say that Roberts does not deny being in the area, although he does deny having started the fire. He was called by Slettom's secretary and asked to come to the appliance store before business hours, he says. He claims she told him that, in spite of the fire that made the store he was renting uninhabitable, he still had to sign a paper canceling his lease. Mr. Slettom and his secretary deny having called Roberts or having requested a meeting."

"They can't possibly think Mr. Roberts just

made that story up, can they?" Trixie asked her brothers.

Mart was speechless for a change, and Brian shook his head as if refusing to hazard a guess on what the police might or might not do. Before he could add a comment, Helen Belden called him to the phone.

He was gone for just a few moments, but when he came back, his face was pale and sick-looking. "That was one of my T-shirt customers," he said, his voice strained. "He called to cancel an order for twenty-five shirts."

"Oh, Brian, that's too bad," Trixie said automatically. Then she realized that her brother was over-reacting to the loss of one small sale. "Why did he cancel?" she asked.

"Why do you think?" Brian snapped. "He said it looks to him as though Nicholas Roberts is guilty, after all, and he doesn't want to do business with an arsonist."

"What!" Trixie shrieked. "But that's ridiculous!"

"I agree," Brian said. "I even told him so, as politely as I could. But he doesn't know Mr. Roberts, or Nick, so he doesn't understand how ridiculous it is."

The conversation was interrupted again. This

time Mart was called to the phone. Trixie felt her stomach beginning to churn. *Please, please let it be something else*, she thought. *A new order, or even just an invitation to a dumb party — anything but another cancellation.*

It was another cancellation, though. Trixie and Brian knew that before Mart spoke. They could tell it by the way his shoulders slumped as he walked across the room, and by the way he sat down heavily in his chair.

"Who and how many?" Brian asked quietly.

"Shorty's Shoe Shop. Twenty shirts and twenty caps," Mart said simply.

"What did they say?" Trixie asked.

"There's no need for me to repeat the conversation," Mart told her. "Basically, it was identical to Brian's."

Trixie sighed, then jumped as the telephone began to ring again. She knew it was her turn before she heard her mother call, "Trixie!" She got up from the table and went to the phone.

"This is Jan Carlson," the voice said. "I ordered some caps for our horseshoe tournament."

"I remember," Trixie said. She tried to keep the coldness out of her voice, but she wasn't going to make it easier for the man to cancel his order.

"I've been thinking it over, and it seems like a

lot of money to spend. It's just a little family picnic, after all. Could I — I'd like to cancel my order." The last sentence came out all in a rush.

"All right," Trixie said. "Consider it canceled."

"I-I'm sorry," the man said.

Trixie had to admit that he sounded as if he
meant it. But she couldn't tell the man that it was
all right. "Good-bye," she said simply.

She went back to the table determined to tell
her brothers what she'd seen the night before in
the alley behind Roberts's store. But before she
could speak, Brian was again called to the phone.

When he stood up, Trixie stood up at the same
time. "All right," she said. "That does it." Without
another word of explanation, she slammed out of
the house, dragged her bike out of the garage, and
rode as fast as she could to the Manor House.
When Celia let her in, she ran up the stairs to Honey's room two at a time. "Come on, Honey," she
said. "We're going to the police!"

Honey sat up on the bed, at the same time making hasty brushing motions under her eyes.

She's been crying, Trixie thought. Aloud she
asked, "Have you had customers canceling
orders?"

Honey nodded. "T-They say they think Mr.
Roberts is guilty. T-They say they d-don't want to

do business with s-someone like that." Honey's voice was trembling.

"The same thing happened to us," Trixie said. "That's why I want to go downtown and tell the police about seeing Jane Dix-Strauss in the alley last night."

Trixie half-expected her friend to protest as she had the night before. Today, though, Honey seemed more than willing to go along with the plan. "Let's go," Honey said firmly, and she led Trixie out the door.

The two girls rode in silence into Sleepyside. Both wanted to ride as quickly as they could, and Trixie wanted to rehearse her speech, as well.

They parked their bikes outside the police station and walked in. Trixie took in the waiting room with a sweeping glance, and saw Mr. Slettom sitting there. He was wearing another loud and lively sports coat, but he was looking sad and uncomfortable. Leaning casually against a wall not far away was Jane Dix-Strauss. *Oh, woe*, Trixie thought. *I was hoping there would be no one here, especially not her.* Wanting to turn and run, she forced herself to march up to the reception desk instead. "I'd like to speak to Sergeant Molinson," she said.

"Your name?" asked the receptionist.

"Trixie Belden," she said.

"I'll tell him you're here," the woman said. She dialed a two-digit number and spoke Trixie's name into the receiver. "He says to wait," she told Trixie.

Trixie stood for a moment leaning against the high reception counter. She didn't want to turn around. Her mental rehearsal for this scene hadn't included having to wait in a room with the woman she was about to accuse of hiring an arsonist — and the man whose stores the arsonist had burned!

Honey, always better in social situations, put her arm through Trixie's. "Come on," she said, turning her friend away from the counter and leading her to a row of chairs along the wall opposite Mr. Slettom.

The girls sat with their hands folded in their laps and their heads lowered. It was as if they hoped that by not looking at anyone, they could make themselves invisible. A voice speaking nearby told them the plan hadn't worked.

"You girls are friends of young Nick Roberts, aren't you?" the voice asked.

Trixie looked up and saw that Mr. Slettom had walked over to stand near them.

"Too bad," Mr. Slettom said, shaking his head.

"Too bad we're Nick's friends?" Trixie asked in confusion.

"No, no, no — too bad Roberts set this second

fire. He would have gotten away with the first one, if he just hadn't pushed it."

"Y-You mean you think Mr. Roberts is guilty?" Trixie asked fearfully.

"Well, it's obvious, isn't it?" Mr. Slettom countered. "You know I thought he was innocent the first time around. Why, I offered him bail, anything he needed. But then —" Mr. Slettom broke off for a moment, shaking his head in the same sad way. "He just pushed it too far."

"But why do you think he set fire to your store?" Trixie asked.

"I wish I knew. Maybe he just has it in for me. Sometimes people get that way, you know, when they've been under a lot of stress. They go looking for someone to blame, someone to get even with for all that's happened."

"But Mr. Roberts's problems were all over by the time the fire started in his store," Trixie protested.

"Unless you figure not being able to move was the final problem — the straw that broke the camel's back, so to speak," Mr. Slettom pointed out.

"Is that what you're going to tell the police?" Trixie asked.

"Of course not," Mr. Slettom said indignantly. "I may not like it that Nicholas Roberts burned down my store, but I'm not trying to make trouble for him. I'll give the police the facts, that's all. And I won't tell *that* one anything." He gestured with his head toward the reporter.

"We're sorry," Honey said. "We didn't mean to sound as though we were accusing you. We're just worried about Mr. Roberts."

"You have every reason to be worried," Mr. Slettom said, his voice sounding sad once again.

"Well, well, well," said another voice nearby. "It's the Belden-Wheeler Detective Agency, come to call on the police. To what do we owe this honor?"

Trixie looked up and saw that Sergeant Molinson had come out of his office. "We have something to tell you," she said.

"Well, what is it?" he demanded.

Trixie looked nervously at Mr. Slettom and then at Jane Dix-Strauss, who was staring at her openly. "Could we — could we go to your office? It's sort of private."

"Trixie Belden, I have two unsolved arsons to investigate, a thousand phone calls to return, and a million other things to take care of. I can't spend all day talking to a couple of teenage detectives. Tell me what's on your mind or be on your way," Sergeant Molinson ordered.

The sergeant was usually good-natured. Today he was obviously strained and showed it. Trixie knew that she had to speak out in public or not be heard at all.

She cleared her throat and said, "Did you know that Jane Dix-Strauss wrote a long article on arson before she came to Sleepyside?"

"No, I didn't, but I'm glad you've cleared up the mystery of her excellent reporting on the subject." Sergeant Molinson was being mockingly polite. "Now, is there anything else?"

Trixie hesitated, her confidence about to desert her. Then she felt Honey's arm slide through her own, and she took courage from her friend's presence. "A couple of weeks ago, I found a button with Jane Dix-Strauss's initials on it in the alley behind Mr. Roberts's store. Then, last night, I saw her behind the store. There was a big man with her, and she handed him an envelope and said she'd call him if she needed anything else." Trixie let the words come out in one long stream. When she was finished, she was out of breath and she felt her pulse pounding in her temples.

Sergeant Molinson looked down at Trixie and Honey for a minute. Then he turned around and barked at Jane Dix-Strauss, "Were you in that alley last night?"

Trixie jumped at the sound of it. Then she realized that Sergeant Molinson had counted on surprise to get an unrehearsed answer.

What the sergeant counted on didn't work, however. Jane Dix-Strauss showed no reaction to being shouted at. Calmly, she pushed herself away from the wall and walked toward the policeman and the two girls. "I think the young woman is making a mistake," she said firmly.

"But, I —" Trixie began to protest, but the sergeant held up his hand to stop her.

"Did you see her behind Roberts's store, too?" he asked Honey.

"No," Honey admitted. "I saw the button, though," she added helpfully.

"Look, girls," Sergeant Molinson said, sounding tired. "I know you want to help your friend Nick Roberts, but this isn't the way to do it. If you say you found Miss Dix-Strauss's button in the alley, I believe you. She might very well have been poking around there, just as Trixie was, and lost a button. But if she says you're mistaken, I'm willing to take her word for it. And I really don't have any more time to waste talking about it." The sergeant turned and walked away, leaving Trixie feeling angry and embarrassed.

"Come on, Honey," she said. She led the way

quickly out of the police station, refusing to look around for fear of seeing Mr. Slettom's sad face or Jane Dix-Strauss's gloating one.

The girls rode back home and parted at the foot of the Belden driveway. "I guess I'd better get to my chores," Trixie said. "I'll have plenty of time to do them now — there's no point even trying to sell T-shirts."

"Do you want to come over when your chores are done?" Honey asked. "You've been too busy to sleep over in simply ages. Miss Trask mentioned it this morning."

Trixie remembered the loneliness she'd felt the night before, when she couldn't confide in her brothers. Now she was even more reluctant to do so, since it would also mean telling them about the humiliation at the police station. "Okay," she said to Honey. "I'll be over right after dinner, if Moms says it's okay."

Mrs. Belden, having heard about the canceled orders, readily agreed to let Trixie spend the night with her friend. Although the afternoon dragged, it did finally pass, and Trixie went back to the Manor House.

By unspoken consent, the girls tried to stay away from the subjects of arson, Mr. Roberts's future, or sales of caps and T-shirts. Every other sub-

ject seemed to remind them of those, though —
even the color scheme Honey had come up with
for the clubhouse and the design she'd sketched
for new shelves.

"It will look wonderful," Trixie said lamely. To
herself she added, *If we ever get the money for it.*

When bedtime finally came, all the suppressed
thoughts came tumbling into Trixie's conscious-
ness. She heard Honey's even breathing and knew
her friend was asleep, but she couldn't follow that
good example. Instead, she tossed and turned. Finally, after midnight, she gave up trying to sleep
and went to stand by the window. The night was
clear and the sky was studded with stars. Trixie
felt some calmness creeping back into her agitated
mind.

The calmness disappeared and her heart
skipped a beat when she saw a shadowy figure en-
ter the Wheelers' stable and pull the door closed
behind it!

12 * The Right Suspect

IN NO MORE THAN TEN SECONDS, it was all over — the shadowy figure was gone, the door was closed, and all was still. What Trixie had seen began to seem like a distant memory. She started to wonder whether she had imagined the whole thing.

I can't be sure, she thought, *but there's only one way to find out.* Noiselessly, she tiptoed over to her clothes, which were piled on a chair. She pulled on her jeans and T-shirt, and carried her tennis shoes. The need to be quiet forced her to move slowly out of the room, down the long hall, and down the stairs.

After what seemed like hours, Trixie reached the front door. She grasped the huge brass knob as firmly as she could and turned it slowly and carefully until she felt the door release. Then she pulled it open, still moving in slow motion, ready to freeze if the door gave the slightest squeak. It didn't. *Of course not*, Trixie thought. *With all those servants, a squeaky door doesn't stand a chance at the Manor House.*

Trixie stepped outside and pulled the door closed behind her. Then she stopped to put on her shoes, hopping around first on one foot and then the other. *Oh, woe*, she thought, *why didn't I just sit down to do this? Because it would have taken extra time, and I'm in such a hurry — so I spend twice as much time trying to keep my balance. When will I ever learn?*

Finally, remarkably, she made it across the path to the stable door without mishap, without the lights suddenly going on in the house behind her — and without the shadowy intruder opening the door to come back out.

Trixie paused for a moment to get a clear mental picture of what lay on the other side of the door. Just inside was the tack room, which ran the full width of the stable. It was a separate room, with a door that led back into the stalls where the horses were kept. The door was usually closed, so there would be no way for Trixie to know whether someone was hiding behind it. There was a small closet in the tack room, too, which was used for Regan's leather repair and carpentry tools. It was another perfect hiding place.

Trixie wiped her clammy hands on the sides of her jeans before she reached out for the handle of the stable door. She'd just have to hope that the intruder was still in the tack room and not trying to hide. Moving fast and taking the intruder by surprise was her best chance.

With that in mind, she yanked the door open and reached for the light switch just to the left. She jumped out of the way of the door as light flooded the tack room.

There was a gasp and a crackle of straw as the intruder whirled around, showing Trixie her astonished and frightened face.

"Jane Dix-Strauss!" Trixie said in a loud whisper. "What are you doing here?"

The young reporter put her hand to her chest and let out a long, whistling breath. "Right at the moment, I'm trying to get my heart to stop doing the tango. You scared the daylights out of me!"

Trixie couldn't believe her ears. Jane Dix-Strauss had *looked* frightened when she'd first turned around, but now she didn't *sound* frightened. "I suppose you'd like me to leave so you can start another fire," Trixie said. "That is, if your friend isn't available to start this one."

That remark, which Trixie had intended to make Jane Dix-Strauss angry, seemed to amuse her instead. There was a hint of a smile on the reporter's face as she said, "My friend, as you call him, isn't going to start a fire here tonight. Neither am I. The real arsonist will, though — unless you scare him away."

"Is that your way of saying you've set a trap for Mr. Roberts?" Trixie demanded.

"Of course not," the reporter said. "Mr. Roberts isn't the arsonist. I've known that from the beginning."

"Then why did you write that article that made him look suspicious?"

"I wrote the facts, because that's my job as a reporter. And the facts that were available *did* make Mr. Roberts look guilty. I tried to get other facts — the ones that would prove he's innocent. If I'd been able to interview Mr. Roberts, I could have asked questions and gotten answers that would have turned the suspicion on the *right* person. But his son told me to get lost — remember?"

"Who is this 'right person'?" Trixie asked, still suspicious.

"You mean you don't know?" Jane Dix-Strauss

asked right back. "You gave me the crucial piece of evidence."

"Your button? How could your button prove that someone else started the fires?" Trixie asked, completely confused.

"I didn't say it was my button," Jane Dix-Strauss said. "In fact, it isn't, and that's why it's crucial."

"Of course, it's your button," Trixie said, growing angry again. "It said JDS right on it. Who else —" She broke off in mid-sentence, and her eyes grew round.

Jane Dix-Strauss nodded a confirmation of what Trixie had just guessed. "Now you know *who*. I'll be happy to explain the *what, when, where,* and *why,* as we journalists say. But not now. If he finds you here, the whole thing will be spoiled. Would you leave now, please?"

Trixie hesitated. Her distrust of Jane Dix-Strauss was fading, but it hadn't disappeared. Her love of a mystery was as strong as ever. Finally, she said, "I'm not leaving."

"O-O-Oh!" The sound came out as a groan, and Jane Dix-Strauss shoved her hands into the pockets of her blazer as if she were afraid of what she might do with them. "All right, stay here — but stay out of sight, would you?"

Trixie looked around for a way of doing that and

decided on the small closet in the corner of the tack room. From there, she wouldn't be able to see what was happening, but at least she could hear. She went into the closet, leaving the door ajar.

The reporter suddenly stuck her head around the door. "One more thing," she said briskly. "Stay out of sight until I tell you otherwise. I'm trying to get evidence that will stand up in court. I know what that evidence is and you don't. If you pop up at the wrong time, the arsonist goes free. You don't want that, do you?"

Trixie shook her head, and the reporter withdrew. There was a click as Jane Dix-Strauss turned off the light, and Trixie found herself in darkness. She could hear the occasional stirring of the horses on the other side of the wall behind her and could smell their rich, pungent aroma.

The quiet darkness seemed to go on forever. Finally, Trixie heard the sound of the door sliding open. Then there was light — not the blinding light of the overhead bulb, but a softer light. *He must have brought a flashlight*, she thought. *Oh, I wonder if it's really him.*

"So, you showed up," a man's voice said.

It sounds like him, Trixie thought, *but I can't be sure*. She felt her heart start to race with nervousness and curiosity. Then she noticed a beam of light cutting through the darkness in the closet. *A hole in the boards!* she thought excitedly. She traced the beam to its source in the wall near the floor. Crouching, she put her eye close to the small hole. At first, all she saw was Jane Dix-Strauss's slender back. The man who had just entered was facing her, and Trixie couldn't see who it was.

"I showed up," Jane Dix-Strauss said. "Did you really think I'd pass up an interview with Sleepyside's only arsonist?"

There was silence in the stable. Trixie could sense the man's anger at the reporter's jibe. He turned away, into Trixie's line of vision.

Trixie put her hand over her mouth to stifle a gasp. *It is! It's Mr. Slettom!* she exclaimed soundlessly.

"I don't remember admitting that I started those fires," the man said.

"No, that's true," Jane Dix-Strauss told him. "Your secretary said that you had some information for me. I guess I just assumed, since she insisted on giving me this information in the middle of the night in an out-of-the-way place, that it was, shall we say, firsthand."

"You're a cagey one, aren't you?" Mr. Slettom asked, without expecting an answer.

"So are you," Jane Dix-Strauss said. "Shifting

the blame onto Nicholas Roberts was especially clever."

"Yeah, well — that's the one thing I'm really sorry about," Slettom said. "Not that the police suspected him — I meant for that to happen. But I never thought it would go this far. Why, they're about to press charges against him."

"You wanted Mr. Roberts suspected just enough so they couldn't suspect you, is that it?" Jane Dix-Strauss asked.

"Yeah, that's it," Mr. Slettom said. "I couldn't let him be arrested or have to stand trial. He's a nice man, with a nice family. I tell you, I was getting pretty nervous. I was afraid I might have to confess to having set those fires myself."

"That's where I came in, is it?" Jane Dix-Strauss said.

Mr. Slettom had been pacing back and forth as he spoke, moving in and out of Trixie's narrow range of vision. Now he stopped and looked back at the reporter in surprise. "You figured that out, too, did you?" he asked. "My, you *are* a clever one."

"Let's see how clever I am," she said. "My guess is that you really got desperate when you heard the Belden girl talking to Sergeant Molinson this morning. When she said she'd found my button in the alley behind the store, you, of course, knew it was really your button, Mr. James D. Slettom. You also knew that I'd know the button wasn't mine, and that I'd soon figure out whose it was.

"But Trixie's accusation gave you an idea, too. You'd cast a little suspicion on me, the way you already had on Mr. Roberts. It would take some of the heat off him, without getting me into serious trouble. Is that how you'd figured it?"

"That's it, almost exactly. I've got to hand it to you." There was genuine admiration in Slettom's voice. "You're too new around here to know it, but that young Belden girl has a reputation for being a pretty good detective. Sergeant Molinson didn't believe her today, but after you're found at the scene of the third fire, he'll reconsider."

"Aren't you worried about the countercharges I'll make against you?" Jane Dix-Strauss asked.

"Well, no," Slettom said slowly. "You see, I don't plan for you to be able to make any countercharges. I guess that's the one place where you figured it wrong — the part about me not getting you into serious trouble. I'm going to have to get you into the worst kind of trouble there is."

"Are you saying you're planning to kill me?" Jane Dix-Strauss asked. Trixie was amazed at the coolness in the reporter's tone.

"Oh, well, that's putting it kind of strong. I'd just say I'm not going to *save* you, once the fire starts."

From her hiding place, Trixie saw Mr. Slettom suddenly raise his arm, then lower it. There was a thud as something hit Jane Dix-Strauss on the head. The reporter seemed to crumple, then dropped out of Trixie's sight.

Mr. Slettom stood for a moment looking down at her. The expression on his face made Trixie's stomach turn. He looked grim and sad and triumphant, all at the same time. Then he bent down and was also lost from Trixie's field of vision.

Not being able to see what was happening, Trixie strained her ears for clues. There were a couple of scraping sounds that were familiar, but she couldn't identify them. Then Mr. Slettom stood up again. Trixie could see him looking down at Jane Dix-Strauss.

"I'm sorry," he said. "I really am. This was the best way — the only way, although I suppose I can't expect you to understand that. Nicholas Roberts has a family that needs him. So do I. You don't. You don't have family, you don't have friends. I know all that, see — I did some interviewing of my own. All you've got is your work, and somebody else will take your place there. So it will all turn out for the best." He hesitated for a moment, as if he really expected her to agree with him.

In the silence, Trixie's other senses once again became more acute. She was conscious of the ache in her muscles from sitting so long without moving. She was conscious of a smell, too — something that hadn't been there before. Suddenly she knew what it was. *Fire! He's set the straw on fire!*

That thought had just come to her when the room suddenly went dark. Panic and confusion flooded through Trixie's mind. Had Mr. Slettom left? In her distraction, she hadn't heard the door close. Should she run for the door? Should she shout for help? What if Mr. Slettom hadn't left. What if he was waiting just outside in the dark, to be sure the fire got a good start, to be sure Jane Dix-Strauss didn't get away. She couldn't let Slettom catch her. He'd make sure she died in the fire, too. It would fit right in with his story — Jane Dix-Strauss would have tried to silence Trixie and accidentally been silenced with her.

Trixie's mind raced through those troubled thoughts as she remained crouched and motionless in the closet. Her ears strained for any sound. All they heard was a crackle that told her the fire was spreading. It would take only moments for it to go out of control in the straw-filled stable.

I have to risk it, she thought. She stood up and was struck by how much stronger the smell of smoke was away from the floor. She opened the door of the closet and walked out. She could see the flickering flames in a pile of straw near the door of the stable. The flames lit the ribbons of smoke that curled upward. They also let Trixie see the too-still figure of Jane Dix-Strauss.

Once again, Trixie was faced with a hard decision. Slettom had, cleverly, set the fire close to the door. If she spent any time trying to rouse the reporter, the way out might be blocked for both of them. Yet, if she left to get help with the fire, she might not be able to get back in — not in time for the unconscious young woman. She could try to put out the fire herself, but if she failed, it would cost two human lives and the lives of all the horses in the stable.

"I'll go for help." Trixie was surprised that she'd spoken out loud. She realized that she had, in fact, spoken to Jane Dix-Strauss. It was a promise, even if the reporter couldn't hear it.

For just a fraction of a second, Trixie felt as if she were frozen in place, with the fire spreading even closer to the door. Then she forced her knees to bend, forced herself to move. She would run from the stable to the Manor House as fast as she could, and pray that someone would hear her shouts.

She saved her shouts, though, as she ran toward the house. She would wait until there was at least a chance that someone would hear her.

When she got to the house, she saw the front door open and two figures appear on the top step. "Jim! Honey!" The cry was one of recognition and of gratitude. "Fire! Help!" She stopped running and half-turned back toward the stable. Her friends stared at her, too stunned to move.

"Hurry!" she shouted. "Get the police! Get the fire department! Go!"

She didn't wait for a response. She needed help, and now she had it. The next thing to do was to help Jane Dix-Strauss.

Trixie ran back into the burning stable.

13 * Who, What, When, Where, and Why

THE FLAMES WERE LEAPING KNEE-HIGH inside the stable, and the smoke had already gotten so thick that Trixie could barely see. Her eyes started to tear as she peered through the smoke. Finally, she spotted the motionless form on the floor.

Trixie took a deep breath and ran toward Jane Dix-Strauss. Her first-aid training told her it was dangerous to move the woman — but the sight and sound and smell of the fire told her it was more dangerous not to. Trixie put her hands under the woman's arms and began to pull.

It seemed to take hours to get to the door. Then, from behind her, Trixie felt the cool touch of fresh air. "We did it!" she said out loud. Her exclamation was answered by a groan from Jane Dix-Strauss.

Trixie was overjoyed that the young reporter was alive. She was happy, too, that the fire in the tack room had not yet raged out of control. Leaving Jane Dix-Strauss on the ground outside the stable, she raced back inside, grabbed a saddle blanket that was slung over a rack, and began beating at the flames. She swung the blanket with all her might, releasing all the fear and anger and frustration that had been pent up inside her during the long period of hiding.

She didn't even know how long she'd been fighting the fire when she saw a movement out of the corner of her eye. She turned her head and saw Honey using another saddle blanket to beat at the fire.

Beyond the tack room door, the horses were whinnying in fear and lashing out with their hooves at the sides of their stalls. *If the fire isn't out soon, they'll destroy themselves,* Trixie thought.

In the distance, she heard the wail of the fire sirens. She looked over at Honey, who signaled with a nod that she had heard them, too. But neither of the girls stopped their vital work until a fire fighter in high boots, long coat, and helmet appeared.

"All right," he said, "we'll take over here. You girls leave now." He took the girls by the arms and led them firmly out of the stable.

Only then did Trixie realize how tired she was, how much her arms ached. She looked down at her hands and saw that the palms had been scraped raw against the rough cloth of the saddle blanket.

Jim came running up to them, and threw his arms around them both. "Are you all right?" he asked.

The girls both nodded. Trixie opened her mouth to speak, but nothing came out of her smoke-parched throat. She tried again, and what came out was a low-pitched croak: "Is Jane all right?"

Jim frowned, and Trixie thought the worst, but he said, "I think she is — or will be. We took her into the house. The doctor should be here soon."

"You were busy," Trixie said, "calling the fire department and the doctor and carrying Jane inside."

"That's the least of it," Jim said. "There's my finest accomplishment right there." He gestured toward the driveway.

Trixie looked and saw what she hadn't noticed before — three squad cars, in addition to the fire truck. Sergeant Molinson was among the policemen who were milling around. More important, though, was the single figure huddled in the back seat of one of the cars.

"Mr. Slettom?" Trixie asked in amazement.

"Mr. Slettom!" Honey exclaimed as her brother nodded. "What is he doing here? What does he have to do with all of this?"

"Absolutely everything," Trixie said.

"I hope that's true," Jim said, grinning in spite of the seriousness of the situation. "Otherwise I'm in big trouble. After you yelled for help, I saw someone standing a few yards down the driveway. He must have been making his escape when he heard you shouting. I'll bet he was horrified to discover there had been another witness. He must have waited around, hoping there'd be a way to get rid of you, too.

"I called to him, and he started to run. So I ran after him and tackled him and held him until the police got here."

"That was wonderful of you!" Honey said proudly.

Jim smiled at his sister. Then his face got serious again. "It wasn't so wonderful to leave you two to fight that fire alone," he said. "I had no idea you'd gone back in until I'd already tackled Slettom. Then there was nothing I could do but wait until the fire department and police showed up."

"Well, anyway, it all worked out just fine," Trixie assured him.

"Oh, did it, now?" a deep voice asked. The three young people turned and saw Sergeant Molinson walking toward them. "Perhaps you'll come in the house and tell me all about it."

Trixie surprised herself by shivering suddenly in the cool evening air. "Going in the house sounds like a good idea, anyway," she said. She turned and led the way inside.

A worried-looking Miss Trask, in bathrobe and slippers that somehow looked as businesslike as her usual tailored suits, met them at the door with hugs and led them into the den. There, Jane Dix-Strauss was propped up on a couch, her hands wrapped around a blue mug. A pot of tea, more mugs, and some cookies were on a tray nearby.

"Are you all right?" Trixie asked.

Jane Dix-Strauss started to nod, then winced and put her hand to her head. "I was a little shaken up on the play, as the sportscasters say. I'm alive, though — thanks to you."

"I'm glad I was able to help," Trixie said as she

poured herself a cup of steaming tea and took two cookies from the tray.

"So the schoolgirl shamus was in the thick of things, as usual," Sergeant Molinson said. "Suppose you tell me what happened."

"They've been through enough for one night," Miss Trask said. She looked ready to tackle the whole Sleepyside police department, not just Sergeant Molinson. "Why don't you leave them alone until tomorrow morning?"

"I really don't mind talking," Jane Dix-Strauss said. "In fact, it's probably a good idea. If I have a concussion, I should do whatever I can to stay awake."

"I don't mind talking, either," Trixie said. "I couldn't possibly calm down for a while — talking might help."

"All right," Miss Trask said reluctantly. "But you'll let them talk, Sergeant — not interrogate them."

"Yes, ma'am," Sergeant Molinson said sheepishly. He looked relieved when the doorbell rang and Miss Trask left the room to answer it. "Now," he said, trying to regain his dignity. "Who wants to start?"

"I suppose I'd better," Jane Dix-Strauss said. "I'd suspected —"

Her story was interrupted by shouts in the hall. "Trixie? Where are you? Are you all right?" Brian and Mart burst through the door, stopping suddenly when they saw the sergeant and the reporter.

"We heard the sirens," Brian said, making his way more cautiously into the room. "We tried to call and couldn't reach anyone, so Moms and Dad sent us over here to make sure everyone was all right."

"We're fine," Trixie assured him, "except that there's a fire in the stable."

"Not any more," Brian told her. "The fire fighters were packing up their hoses as we came in."

"Well, then, everything is terrific," Trixie said. "Sit down. Jane Dix-Strauss is just about to tell us how she figured out that Mr. Slettom was the arsonist."

"Mr. Slettom?" Brian asked, sounding as amazed as Honey had earlier.

"Jane Dix-Strauss?" For Mart, the presence of the once-loathed news reporter was the biggest mystery.

"Listen and learn," Jim said, gesturing toward empty chairs.

"Meanwhile," said Miss Trask dryly, "I'll call

Mr. and Mrs. Belden and tell them that Trixie says everything is terrific."

Trixie's brothers settled down and looked expectantly at Jane Dix-Strauss. The young woman cleared her throat and began again.

"I'd suspected Slettom almost from the first. The Memorial Day arson reminded me immediately of another fire I'd heard about when I was researching for a magazine article. You see, Mr. Slettom started the fire in the basement of the trophy shop so that Mr. Roberts would be suspected. But the real purpose of the arson was to burn down the building next door, which was used as a warehouse by Mr. Slettom.

"I suspect, Sergeant, that if you can find any records that weren't destroyed during the second fire, you'll see that Mr. Slettom claimed to have a huge inventory of new appliances stored in that warehouse. They'll be valued at thousands of dollars and insured for that amount."

"But they weren't new appliances?" Sergeant Molinson guessed.

"No," Jane Dix-Strauss said. "They were old ones, nearly worthless."

"So the idea was to burn down the warehouse and collect the insurance on the inventory shown on paper," Jim said.

Jane Dix-Strauss nodded. "The warehouse was

to burn so completely that the appliances would be heaps of molten metal. No one would be able to tell whether they were new or used, working or useless. But the plan didn't work because Slettom bungled the arson. The building blew up instead of burning down. The old appliances in the warehouse were still identifiable. That led to the second fire."

"You mean Mr. Slettom tried to burn more appliances so he could create another falsified insurance claim?" Mart asked.

"No. The point of the second fire wasn't to burn appliances. It was to burn records," Jane said.

"Of course!" Brian sat forward in his chair. "Mr. Slettom would have created some pretty fancy paperwork for the fake inventory in the warehouse — something convincing enough to collect insurance on. He'd have already destroyed the records of the old appliances, because he wouldn't want an insurance investigator to stumble across them. But when the warehouse blew up instead of burning down, it was the fake ones that were dangerous. They showed new appliances, but the contents of the warehouse could be recognized as *old* ones."

"Couldn't he just throw the phony records out?" Trixie asked.

"Not unless he had something to replace them

with," Brian told her. "But he didn't, because he'd already destroyed the real records. No, he had to come up with some excuse for not having records of the warehouse inventory at all."

"So he staged another fire," Trixie concluded.

Jane Dix-Strauss nodded again. "I was afraid he would, eventually. There was nothing I could do about it, though. Proving arson takes more than suspicions and a good motive. It requires showing exclusive opportunity, which means that no one else *could* have started the fire; or intent, which means that the fire was started on purpose. I hoped to prove one of those by continuing to investigate and looking for evidence. I missed the only real clue, though. Trixie found that."

"The button," Trixie explained as all eyes turned her way.

"So it really was a clue!" Honey exclaimed proudly.

"Would you care to elucidate on the history of this infamous fastener?" Mart asked.

Trixie briefly told Jim and her brothers about finding the gold monogrammed button behind Roberts's store, about assuming that the initials were Jane Dix-Strauss's, and about confronting the reporter and losing the evidence as a result.

"I knew, of course, that it wasn't my button as soon as Trixie handed it to me," Jane said. "I really

don't go in for anything as flashy as monogrammed buttons."

"Mr. Slettom goes in for *everything* flashy,"
Trixie said. "I should have picked up on that."

"I had a big advantage, though," Jane said.
"Slettom and I have the same initials, and that's
the kind of thing a person notices right away.

"Anyway, when Trixie said she'd found the button *under* a brick in the alley, I realized that meant
Slettom must have lost it *before* the fire, when the
bricks came tumbling down."

"Then Mr. Slettom started the second fire and
Mr. Roberts looked even guiltier and I stormed
down to the police station and accused you,"
Trixie said ruefully.

"You what?" Brian asked.

"Our sibling is developing her propensity for
secretive actions," Mart said.

"I was in too much of a hurry to tell you before I
went, and I was too embarrassed when I got back,"
Trixie explained. "The whole thing really blew up
in my face."

"It wasn't a total loss," Jane Dix-Strauss said. "It
was your accusation that brought us all here tonight."

"You're going to have to explain that a little
more thoroughly for those of us who were kept in
the dark," Jim said.

"Well, in front of both me and Slettom, Trixie told the sergeant that I'd written an article on arson two years ago, that a button with my initials on it had been found in the alley behind Roberts's store, and that I'd been seen in the alley talking to a mysterious man the night before the fire at Slettom's store.

"The sergeant didn't think twice about the accusation, but Slettom did. It made Slettom more desperate because he realized I'd know whose initials those really were on the button. It also gave him a way out. He could cast suspicion on me as he already had on Mr. Roberts. He had his secretary call me tonight as she called Mr. Roberts last night. She said she was Honey Wheeler and that she and Trixie Belden had more proof that I was the arsonist. She said she'd tell the police unless I came to the stable to talk it over."

"Why would he ask you to meet him in the stable?" Brian asked.

"Where else?" Jane Dix-Strauss countered. "If two fourteen-year-olds want to arrange a secret meeting, they can't say, 'Come on over and have my mother show you to my room.' They also can't risk trying to get too far from home. That part, at least, made perfect sense."

"It's still a pretty flimsy story," Sergeant Molinson said.

"I thought so," Jane Dix-Strauss agreed. "The secretary didn't do a very good job of sounding like a fourteen-year-old, either. But Mr. Slettom isn't a professional criminal, and I think we can assume he was just desperate enough to try anything. If it hadn't worked, he would have tried something else."

"There was another good reason for him to think it would work," Trixie said. "After all, it wasn't important for you to believe the story. It was just important for you to show up. Anyone who's had anything to do with you would know you'd show up after a phone call like that. If you were suspicious, you'd be even *more* likely to show up."

Jane Dix-Strauss laughed out loud. "I see I've already made my reputation here in Sleepyside," she said.

"If you knew I wasn't the one who called you, then you must have known you were walking into a trap," Honey said. "That's awfully brave."

"In light of what happened, I'd say it was pretty foolhardy," Jane confessed. "I knew it was a trap, but not that kind of trap. I thought Slettom would just happen by, find me in the stable, start the fire, and then haul me off to the police to accuse me of having set it. I really didn't suspect I was in danger or I never would have come to the stable alone."

"You should have brought that big man you were with in the alley. He'd protect you. Who was he, by the way?" Trixie asked the question with exaggerated casualness.

Jane Dix-Strauss cast a sidelong glance at Sergeant Molinson. Then, with a sigh, she said, "I guess I might as well confess. It's bound to come out eventually.

"You were more right than you knew, Trixie. The man I was with was a practicing arsonist, and the envelope I handed him did have money in it."

There was a round of exclamations, and Jane paused to let the excitement subside before she continued. "He was a source that I'd used in my other arson story. When I got suspicious about the first fire, I called him in for an opinion. He confirmed my suspicions, and I paid him for his — um — professional expertise."

"I suppose the name and whereabouts of this skilled professional are confidential information," Sergeant Molinson said resignedly.

"That's right," Jane Dix-Strauss said. She spoke softly, but there was a defiant look in her eye.

"So you lied when you said Trixie hadn't seen you behind the building," Molinson said.

"I didn't lie, and I didn't say Trixie hadn't seen me behind the building. I said that Trixie was making a mistake, and she was. Accusing me with Slettom standing only ten feet away was a *big* mistake."

"One that almost cost you your life," Trixie said regretfully.

"Oh, come on," Jane said. "It wasn't *that* close a call. I've had worse."

"I'll bet you have," Trixie said admiringly. "That's another thing that made me suspicious of you. You've written stories for big magazines. How come you're working for a little paper like the *Sun*?"

"I like to eat!" Jane retorted. "Sure, I've published some big stories — maybe one every year or two. That's actually a successful free-lance career, but it isn't much in the way of money. I finally decided I wanted a little security. That's why I came here."

"Security!" Sergeant Molinson snorted. "Chasing around after arsonists and using that regular paycheck of yours to pay off other arsonists. That's what you call security, I suppose!"

Jane Dix-Strauss laughed again. "Yes, I suppose

that *is* what I call security, although I'll grant you it wouldn't be the ideal for most people."

"I hope it's ideal for you," Trixie said. "I mean, I really hope you'll stay in Sleepyside."

"I like it pretty well so far," Jane Dix-Strauss said. "I realize, though, that there won't always be as much excitement as there's been in the past month."

"Well, if it's excitement you're looking for, you've fallen in with the right crowd," Sergeant Molinson said. "Trixie and her chums are always at the center of whatever is going on in these parts."

"Oh, he's just exaggerating," Trixie said modestly.

"Sure," Jim said. "The fact that Trixie was trapped with you in a burning building tonight, dragged you to safety, and stayed to help put out the fire is far from commonplace. I'd say nothing similar has happened for a couple of months, at least."

Trixie turned to stick out her tongue at Jim and surprised him by yawning broadly in his face, instead. "Anyway," she said dreamily, sinking back in her chair, "everything worked out just fine. Things always do, you know."

"That's right," Honey agreed. "The real arsonist

has been caught, which means that Mr. Roberts will be cleared, which means that we'll be able to sell lots of T-shirts and build lots of shelves."

"T-shirts? Shelves? I'm afraid that you lost me on that last curve," Jane said.

Briefly, fighting back sleep, Trixie explained about their plan to sell T-shirts and caps, thereby helping Mr. Roberts and themselves at the same time.

"Some reporter I am," Jane said. "I had no idea all this was happening. It sounds like a page one story to me — and it will be, as soon as I can sit up at a typewriter again."

"Really?" Honey asked. "You'll write about us in the *Sun*?"

"Absolutely. I have a good photo to use with the story, too, as I recall."

Honey giggled. "That's right. I remember when your flash went off and set off Trixie's temper along with it."

"That was before," Trixie said huffily. "I'm ready to forget the past and think about the future. Why, if Jane writes about us, we'll get orders for hundreds and hundreds of T-shirts. We won't have to settle for paint and shelves. We can have wallpaper and carpet and a fireplace and —"

"Whoa!" Brian said. "We'd better get you home

to bed. You're already dreaming."

"I am not," Trixie protested, but she let Brian pull her to her feet and guide her out of the room.

At the door, the Beldens met the doctor coming in, carrying his black bag. "Take good care of Jane," Trixie told him. "She has an important story to write."

"This is the star of the story right here," Brian said to the slightly startled doctor.

"I'm not the star," Trixie said. "All the Bob-Whites are." *And that's just the way it should be,* she thought as she and her brothers walked out into the clear summer night, *forever and ever.*